Love
in Korea

By: Misbah Zaidi

Dearest Rijul,

I hope you enjoyed reading the book!
Lets see what comes next!
I love you dearly.
Thank you for all your support!
xoxo

Copyright Page

Edited by: Sarah Lamb
Cover by: Emily's World of Design

Visit: www.fallinginloveinkorea.com
Contact the author at: fallinginloveinkorea@gmail.com

Dedication

This book is dedicated to those affected by Covid-19. I hope this brings joy to everyone during this difficult time.

CHAPTER ONE

The Mistake

"The epithelium consists of the apical and the basal surface…" the lecture about epithelial tissues is going in one ear and out the other. I've already heard this about a million times, and I don't know why exactly my professor was repeating material after we've finished all of our exams. I was just ready to get out of this anatomy class and snuggle up in my bed for the rest of the winter break. It's not that I'm sick of PA school - physician assistant program - but I'm not entirely the happiest either as of right now. Finishing my first semester of grad school went well IF you consider studying sixteen hours a day while crying for ten minutes after each hour NOT miserable at all. After class, I meet up with just about the greatest person I know- my best friend Jace. He's a first-year medical student, while I am a first-year PA student at USC. During undergrad, we would fantasize about attending graduate schools together, little did we know that would become a reality.

Jace is standing by the Trojan horse. He's very hard to miss. He has broad shoulders, is relatively tall compared to me standing at 5' 5. He looks majestic standing under the sunlight, making his olive tone skin shine even brighter. He oozes the beauty of a fine Latino man. I've always been jealous of how put together he always is, even in the middle of finals. His black, wavy hair matches perfectly with his distinctive modelesque eyebrows.

"What's up, baby girl? Why do you look like you haven't showered in years?" Jace laughs as he's giving me the hug that I desperately need. He looks at my baggy, grey sweatpants and oversized black sweatshirt, all tied in with my long, black mess of hair that's in a bun.

"That's because I haven't. Honestly, I don't even remember the last time I washed my hair."

"Well, first off...EW! That's very unlike you, and second of all, I think that plant was alive before you walked by it." We both look at the plant behind me and laugh. "Now let's go before you kill the Trojan horse as well."

As we head back to our apartment, we see a poster of this new K-Pop group that Jace is currently obsessed with.

"ZARA, LOOK! Ah, it's NOWus's poster from their new song! They're all so hot, but isn't AJ so dreamy?!" He stops me from taking a step forward and forcefully turns my head to look at it. I didn't really look, my attention was on a girl who was trying to take a selfie with the poster. It was actually quite funny because she was getting frustrated that the poster was just out of her picture frame.

"I guess so, how can you be so obsessed with someone you don't even know?" I genuinely question how people can be in these parasocial relationships with celebrities.

"Well, why not? Zara, I can guarantee one of my kidneys that AJ is better than all the guys you have been interested in. Plus, he's funny, one quality that all the guys you've liked have lacked."

"Ouch, what are you trying to say, I go for guys who lack a personality?!" I look at him with genuine concern.

"Yes. That is exactly what I'm saying. You haven't had the best quality of people around you, besides me of course."

Jace isn't exactly wrong. My standards when it comes to men have gone down so low in the past twenty-five years of my life, that just asking how my day has been merits them a gold medal for being the best boyfriend.

When we get to our apartment, Jace immediately gestures to the shower. "GO! Get in the shower, and make sure you scrub every crevice of your body. We are going out tonight to celebrate ending the first semester of grad school without hurting anybody."

"Ah, why! Can we just stay in, please?" Just the thought of getting ready is giving me a headache. I just don't have the energy to be all cute and perky.

"Zara, are you eighty years old?"

"No…" I look down, rolling my eyes because I know he's about to give a speech about how young we are and we can lay in bed once we are old and dying.

"We are young and mobile. Why in the world would we stay home, and watch T.V. when the world is our oyster, just waiting to be eaten?"

Jace should have gone to acting school instead of medical, he's so dramatic.

"I don't like oysters," I reply.

"Today you do. Go shower, get ready. Wear a dress so people know you're not a little boy!" He yells out as I make my way to the shower.

I get out of the shower, staring critically at the reflection in the mirror as I force the brush through my tangled hair. I'm surprised by how long my hair has gotten. I'm thinner since I haven't been eating properly. My skin is still that golden, caramel tone but just with a touch of death. My brown eyes seem bigger than usual because my face has gotten slimmer. Even my nose seems pointier than before. I slather on a face mask, hoping somehow it would make my tiredness go away and bring some life back into my skin.

Ah, these first world problems. I don't have that many problems, honestly. Just abandonment issues, trust issues, ignoring my mental health…just your average Muslim, Pakistani girl problems. I developed this facade of being a diligent student and obedient daughter growing up in a moderate Muslim household, but I definitely have broken a couple of rules here and there, especially back in college. I'm glad I did, because now in grad school, I cannot even breathe without memorizing a medical term.

I grab my speaker and play "Come My Way" by PLVTI-NUM, falling back on the bed and closing my eyes. While my mask is drying, I decide to take a quick nap and slip into a dream. I see myself dancing to this song at a bar, but I'm not dancing by myself...I'm grinding against a guy. A guy who can move to the music, placing his strong, veiny hands on my hips, slowly moving them down to my legs, and then...

"ZARA, wake the hell up or I swear on Jupiter, I will drag you out of this bed and throw you in front of our neighbors!" I wake up with my heart pounding and an intense desire to kill Jace for waking me up right at the climax of my dream.

"I literally was dreaming about dancing with my dream guy to this song, and you ruined it."

"Good, now let's go find you a real life dream boy. Wash your mask, wear this dress I picked out for you and let's get this party started!"

After I wash my face, I put on the dress he picked out for me, and am horrified when I see myself in the mirror.

"Jace, I can literally see my insides through this dress. Why is it so tight?! It doesn't even cover my knees, and you know how much I hate my legs. Everyone's going to think I haven't hit puberty yet. I look like Jack Skellington on meth right now."

"No, no you don't. You need to show off your curves so men know they are dealing with a twenty-five-year-old woman, not a twelve-year-old boy."

"Okay, fine but I am wearing a plaid shirt on top and some tights or else my dead body will not leave this apartment."

4

"Oh my God, why do you have to be so dramatic! You need to live out your youthful body before you have children. Mark my words, you will wish that you had listened to me. And you know what I am going to say?"

"What?"

"I TOLD YOU SO! Okay, I got a shot ready for you on the kitchen counter. Here's your mascara and flutter those long eyelashes of yours. We need to catch a man in those." He laughs, heading towards the kitchen.

Twisting open the cap, I started applying mascara but I'm failing to apply it properly because I keep thinking about my dream. There is no way I would ever dance with a guy like that unless there's an asteroid that poses a threat to Earth and the only way to stop it is for me to dirty dance with a guy. Jesus, I need a life.

"Aye, let's drink!"Jace very enthusiastically sticks his head in and hands me a shot glass, which seems as though death is at the bottom of it. "Drink." He looks down at the shot glass and then back at me.

Gulping the shot, I gag. "This is absolutely disgusting. Just reminds me why I started drinking so late in life. This is pure poison."

"Poison that makes you live a little," he raises his eyebrows. " Are you ready to head out? I was thinking about going to Traditions."

"Traditions it is."

***

We get to Traditions and it is jam packed.

"Looks like there's a lot of meat in the house! Let's find ourselves a meal." Jace smirks. We head straight to the bar. I had to make my way through all these tall USC boys, consistently saying 'sorry' and 'excuse me'.

"Two shots, please," Jace asks the bartender. I see him checking her out.

"You know, Jace. You're all talk. You give me so much crap for not being bold enough to talk to guys, but you yourself cannot even go up to a man or a woman!"

"That is definitely not true. I have more ovaries than you," he scoffs. "Dare me."

"Alright, tell that bartender you think she's cute. You won't."

"Bet." Jace hates being challenged, and I know that so well. Hence why I take advantage of it for my own entertainment. "Hey, I'm trying to make a point to my friend here but I just wanted to tell you that I think you're absolutely gorgeous." He shines his signature smile at her- his trademark move is that he'll look into your eyes while complimenting you, and then looks at your lips right after. He's such a show-off.

She looks at him with the shyest smile you have ever seen and says," Well, you made your point quite clear. You're not so bad yourself." They both start staring at each other, flirting with their eyes. "This one is on the house." She slides over four shots.

"Oh, there is no way in hell I am drinking these, Jace," I protest.

"You're drinking three of these, and then you're cut off for the night. I've been drinking more than you. I gotta be some-what sober to take care of your ass."

"I hate you and I hope a bird shits on your head tomorrow." A mischievous smile brightens his evil face. Oh no, I feel like he's about to do something crazy.

"Hi everyone!" he shouts. Everyone that is around us stops talking and looks at him. "My best friend here just finished her first semester of PA school and we are out here to celebrate but she's being a bore and not drinking. Who here will help me get her drunk?!"

6

They all start cheering and chanting 'drink, drink!'. Kill me now. I look at Jace with the most hateful look I can muster. Telepathically I tell him that I will murder him later on. I take the shot and they start cheering. I take two more, they cheer louder! I start to feel the alcohol kicking in, giving me a great buzz.

"One more!" I yell out.

"This one is on me!" Someone shouts and the bartender hands me another one.

I can see Jace laughing, but I'm not even mad anymore. In fact, I want to dance. I grab him, and we hit the dance floor. As we are dancing to Drakes' song 'MIA', I get more and more buzzed. Jace's face becomes a little bit blurry and I start seeing two of him.

***

I wake up in the middle of our living room. The brutal rays of the sun tickled the shit out of my eyes, forcing me to wake up. My clothes are on from last night, and there is a bag with puke right next to me. What the hell happened?! I get up with the biggest headache I have had in a really, really long time. There are two empty bottles of wine on the kitchen counter and two wine glasses. Crap, did we drink more?

Stumbling, I walk around, only to discover a painful stabbing in my ankle. Did I get into a fight last night, or hit by a hammer?! I start looking around for Jace and cannot find him anywhere. He's not in his room or mine. As I'm in my room - trying to find my phone - I hear him snoring. At first, I can't figure out where it is coming from, but the closer I get to my bathroom the snoring gets louder. I find him in the tub, fully clothed with his mouth wide open. Though I was in a lot of pain, that managed to make me laugh. I turn on the faucet because I'm feeling a little vengeful and also, I want to figure out what the heck happened last night.

"ZARA, WHAT THE HELL!" he tries to get out another word, but water fills his mouth. I turn off the faucet and try to help him up, but his menacing self hugs me so now all of my clothes are wet.

"Jace, you are on my bad list right now!"

"Why the hell wouldn't you just wake me up, instead of trying to drown me like a serial killer?! I swear for a second there I thought I was in an Alfred Hitchcock movie."

"BECAUSE YOU DESERVE IT. I think I blacked out last night because of your speech!"

He stops and laughs as he remembers. "Oh yeah, that was pretty fun." He leaves my bathroom to go to his. I take a quick shower, trying to render any sort of memory.

I come outside to see him in the kitchen pouring orange juice and coffee for us.

"What do you remember from last night?" I ask him.

"Honestly, not much. I remember you dancing to Drakes' song, and then you started getting sloppy." He hands me a mug with black coffee.

"Sloppy?"

"Yeah, you started making out with SO many guys! I wanted you to find one guy, not try all of them!"

The horror that went through my body at the moment is indescribable. "What do you mean?! And you let that happen?!"

"I'm just messing with you. You couldn't stand at one point, so I called an Uber. As we were getting in the car, you slammed the door on your ankle."

Ah, that's why my ankle was in so much pain.

"We came home. But...," he pauses. "We drank more when we got home and I think I may have convinced you that it would be a good idea."

"I'm actually going to hell." I take a sip of my coffee. I can hear the sheer disappointment of my parent's voices in my head.

"It seemed like you were having a great time, Zara! I haven't seen you let loose like that in like, forever! Don't be so hard on yourself. You didn't kill anyone...that we remember of."

"Yeah, just my liver." The thought of vodka was making me gag. "Do you remember anything once we started drinking the wine at home?"

"You know what, I think we were watching some music videos. Oh, yeah!" He says with a brief pause. "We were watching GOT7's and NOWus's music videos. I just remember a little bit after that."

We grab the orange juice and coffee and head to our living room.

"Why is my laptop and wallet outside?" I ask him. "Only you can know since I apparently suffered through amnesia last night."

"I think you were buying something. Probably the last shred of dignity left in your life." I try not to laugh because I'm still mad at him, but I can't help it.

We turn on the T.V. and go on YouTube. The last thing searched was a horrible misspelled sentence that I think was supposed to be 'traveling to South Korea'.

"Did you look this up?" I ask.

"Uhh...I don't remember, honestly." He gets up and heads to his room. I turn the T.V. off and open up my laptop. Right before I hit 'Enter' to log onto my computer, I see him running out of his room frantically.

"WAIT. Don't open your laptop!" He grabs my laptop out of my hands and runs off to his room.

"What is the matter with you?!" I tackle him onto his bed, trying to grab my laptop.

"I think I remember something, and I'm so afraid of it being true!"

"Oh God, what do you mean?!" The worst possible scenarios are going through my head. Jesus, did I buy something really inappropriate?! Did I buy something off of the dark web?

"I just don't think it's the best idea right now to discuss this. I say this because I think you might actually commit a homicide, ME being the victim!"

I get off of him. I smile and ask him very gently to give back my laptop. "I swear, I won't be mad." I think he can sense the fakeness coming out of my voice because he shakes his head.

"I know you're being fake right now. You just want your laptop back."

"No, I promise. I'm calm, I just want to check my emails." I was trying so hard to keep myself from turning into The Hulk.

"Okay, listen. Before anything happens, I just want you to know that I love you."

"I love you, too." Could I be any more fake right now?!

"Yeah. Remember that." He hands over my laptop. We both sit down on his bed. I can see him watching me from the corner of his eye. I don't think I've ever sensed so much fear coming from him before. I type in my password and hit 'Enter'. The first thing that pops up is a confirmation email.

I read out loud. "This is a confirmation email regarding your purchase," I see Jace rolling into a ball, planting his face into his hands. I look back onto my screen and read more. My eyes widen. My heart races a million beats per minute. I get that feeling right before you're about to puke your lungs out. The coffee, the juice, and the vodka from last night come directly up and out of my mouth, into Jace's trash can. Am I reading this right?

"The following are eTickets to South Korea. You're all set for your trip!"

CHAPTER TWO

Fixing The Mistake

"JACE. What?! How the, what the, what are we going to do? What if my Dad sees the charges? How in the world did this happen? Was this your stupid idea?" I am infuriated and can't seem to speak in complete sentences. I'm panicking, thinking about what my parents will say. Oh God, I just want the ground to open up and swallow me whole. I throw my laptop on his bed, and start pacing in his room.

"Remember, you said you loved me no matter what happened! I don't know what else to say but I'm sorry. You freaking out is making me freak out!"

"Oh, Jace. Of course I still love you. I just want to rip your limbs off and feed them to vultures!"

"Zara, okay just breathe. Come here, sit down next to me."

"JACE!" I am so frustrated that he still won't take this seriously. "My Dad checks the statements very religiously. He's going to see I made a two thousand dollar charge on freaking plane tickets!"

As I am yelling at him, I realize I should probably check which credit card was used. There is one card that only I have access to and my Dad doesn't know about it. I open my laptop back up to check the purchase details. In the back of my head, I'm praying I used my card and not my Dad's. "Oh thank God, I used my card." The relief that I felt at that moment was better than getting my first acceptance letter to PA school. "We can still cancel these tickets."

"Okay, listen. This might not be such a bad idea."

Is he serious right now? Not such a bad idea?!

"Yeah, it's not a bad idea till my parents find my dead body in a black body bag because God forbid our plane crashes, and they get a call from the coroner that their idiot of a daughter got on a plane to South Korea, and God was like JUST KIDDING! And now, I've killed myself and all of the innocent passengers."

"Okay, first off...Don't bring God into this. Secondly, look, you can just tell your parents you're staying behind another week to hang out with friends since you didn't get to see them as much this semester." That actually sounded tempting for half a second. "Maybe this is a blessing in disguise."

"It's more like the Grim Reaper in disguise."

"Zara, all I'm saying is that maybe we gotta live a little. Maybe this mistake could turn out to be the best trip of our lives. Maybe it changes our lives! Well, maybe not our whole life, but to a point where it would bring us great joy when we look back on it in a couple years."

He can be quite convincing when he needs to be. Actually, now that I think about it, he should have gone to law school.

The muscles in my face start to relax, but I'm not trying to show too much emotion because I don't want to give him the idea that I might be slightly convinced. "Okay, well, do you have a plan?"

"Right now? Not a solid one, but if you give me like an hour, I think I can come up with a great one. One that also won't make your parents suspicious."

"If your plan seems fitting, then I might consider this trip. So, come up with the best plan that any human has ever come up with."

I head back to my room and lie down. I can't help but smile just a little. I mean, the thought of traveling, being on the plane, seeing new sights, trying new foods...it was getting me really excited. The more I thought about it, the more I was convinced that this might be the best mistake we have ever made. However, I don't want to get my hopes up in case it doesn't work. If I were going to a city close by, I don't think I would be as concerned about my parents finding out. This is literally traveling across oceans. What if they want me home? What if they drive down to surprise me, only to discover I am not there? Crap, what if they decide to wait for me till I get home. They'd be waiting for a couple of days! Once these thoughts come flooding in, I immediately get up to find Jace, who is now in the living room.

"Jace, if you have come up with a plan...even though it has been only ten minutes, don't tell me. This is not happening. We gotta figure out a way to cancel these tickets. When is our flight anyways?" I forgot to check the flight date and time in the midst of my freak out.

"Uhh..funny you should ask," he replies. "It's tomorrow, and our returning flight will be a week from tomorrow, a day before Christmas Eve."

"Tomorrow? TOMORROW? How the hell are we going to pull this off? Jace, what will I tell my parents? They don't let me travel to another state alone, and to another continent... WITHOUT THEM, is out of the question! Like, you do understand why I am freaking out, right? Because it seems as though you're not quite grasping this concept." I grab one of our bar stools and sit because I feel like I'm about to faint.

"Yes, I understand," he replies very calmly. "Call your parents right now and tell them you're having some friends staying over for a week. This will ensure that they won't come because they wouldn't want to intrude, and they won't call you as much. I know your parents, trust me."

Honestly, I still wasn't feeling too great about lying to my parents, but I mean...I kind of was on board with it. He grabs my phone, sits down next to me on a bar stool and hands it to me.

"Call them. I'll talk to them if you start to get nervous. I promise, I won't let anything bad happen, okay?" He grabs my face and kisses my forehead. It actually made me feel better.

I take a couple of deep breaths, go into my call log and click on 'Dad'. It starts to ring, and that's when my heart rate raises back up.

"Hello?"

"Hi, Dad!" Jesus, what was that?! I don't answer the phone like that normally! I start to freak out thinking he probably could sense that I'm about to straight up lie to him.

"Hi Zara beta, how was your night?"

Boy, if only I could tell you. You'd be SO proud.

"It was good, Dad. Jace and I just stayed home and watched a documentary about...uhh, aliens." Gosh, couldn't I say something else?!

"Aliens, huh? Which documentary? I'll watch it, too." He knows. I can sense he knows I'm lying.

"Uhh, it's called...," I look at Jace for an answer. He mouths out 'Unacknowledged'. "Unacknowledged. It's called 'Unacknowledged', a great documentary." I give myself a little credit there. I managed to say it without my voice cracking.

"Oh, great. When are you coming home?" He asks.

Right about now, I'm losing my calm. Shit, how do I say it? I look at Jace, and right when I'm about to say something, he takes my phone from me. "Hi, Uncle Adil! It's Jace." I won't lie, I felt a sense of relief.

"Hello, Jace! It's so nice to hear from you. How were your exams?"

"They were great, Uncle. I wanted to ask you something. Is it okay if Zara stays back for a week? Some of our friends wanted to come and stay with us and hang out since we haven't seen them in such a long time. We've been studying SO much, and just need a little break. Is it okay?" Jace looks at me and gives me a little wink. He knows exactly what he's doing.

On cue, my Dad replies back with, " Of course! You two have a good time, you guys deserve it." That was actually quite surprising to me. I didn't think my Dad would agree with it that quickly. Usually, it takes some convincing.

"Thank you so much, Uncle! Here's Zara." He hands me back my phone with the biggest grin on his face.

"Hi, Dad. Thanks for letting me stay for a bit. I promise I'll come as soon as I get back." Shit, I messed up! Jace was leaving the room but as soon as he heard me say that, he stopped and turned around with a worried look on his face.

"Get back? From where?" My dad asks with a very suspicious tone.

I laugh nervously. "I mean, when my friends leave. Gosh, I need some sleep. I haven't slept a lot in the past few days, so I haven't been quite alert." Yes, I saved myself again!

"Ah, well, you need to get some rest, Zara. I have to go but I will call you tomorrow. I love you, take care."

"Love you, too!" I hang up. Jace is standing at the doorway with a smile on his face.

"Say it!" He shouts.

"Say what, you psycho?"

"Say I saved the day."

Ha! He wishes.

"Yeah, no. I feel like I saved the day." He raises his eyebrows. I mean, he technically saved the day by talking to my Dad and convincing him. I was the one who messed up a few times. "Alright, you saved the day." I answer back in defeat. I couldn't help but smile and honestly...I was starting to get so excited.

"YES, thank you! Alright, we gotta go shopping right now and pack. Gah! We are going to Korea!"

"South. South Korea." I correct him.

15

He has an irritated look on his face. "No, I meant North. Of course I meant South Korea! Unless you have a death wish that I don't know about."

"No..."

"Okay then, don't be know-it-all and ruin my excitement. Get ready. We'll leave in about ten minutes." He grabs me off of the bar stool, and takes me to my room.

I find it funny that as a twenty-five year old, I am still afraid of my parents. I mean, I am a full grown woman! Maybe not physically, but nonetheless, a grown woman. Others my age don't even tell their parents about anything they do. Hell, others even move out at eighteen! I think if my parents had a choice, they'd want me to live with them during school as well. That's a 'perk' of being South Asian. You're basically forever age three in your parent's eyes, and incapable of making any decisions for yourself. My parents are strict, but not strict at the same time. They allowed me to live with Jace for grad school, but even that took days of convincing. I think the only reason they even agreed to it is for my safety. They were concerned about me living alone in LA, especially in this area where crime rates are a little high. It's funny though, when desi aunties and uncles at social gatherings ask who I live with-because somehow they believe it's their right to know what's happening in everyone's personal lives-my parents tell them it's a girl from my program. I don't think people in my community can grasp that concept. A girl, and a guy living together?! They MUST be dating. No, no! Secretly married! They have this talent of fabricating stories from one simple truth, stretching and molding them into elaborative rumors. I swear, if desi people used that same creativity elsewhere, life would be a better place for all of us. Thankfully, my parents aren't anything like them. They're a little lenient and broad minded, but they still worry about our image in the community .'What will people say?' the one question every brown kid has heard...and one that has broken many hearts, including mine.

16

While I'd say I'm quite blessed, I am still deathly afraid of disappointing them.

We end up going to CVS to pick up some travel essentials, and to a couple of stores to pick out a hefty jacket. Apparently it's incredibly cold around this time of year, which is perfect because I absolutely love the cold weather. Honestly, I feel as if I should have been born in a colder state, not California. There is just something about the cold weather. Sitting by the fireplace, it's raining outside, eating warm cookies with milk, and watching a movie...like, doesn't that sound just so relaxing?

We get back home and immediately I begin to pack. I grab my large suitcase, and start coming up with different outfits that I might wear. Jace walks in and I know he's about to give his two cents once he sees all of my NASA shirts laid out.

"Seriously? You're going to bring your NASA shirts...to Korea?!"

"South. South Korea!" I correct him again. He chooses to ignore me this time, and grabs five out of the six NASA shirts I laid out and puts them back into my closet.

"You can only bring one. People might actually think you're an alien. Your big ass eyes already fit the description." He laughs. "Do you need help choosing your outfits?"

"Uhh, not really?" I definitely needed help.

"Say no more. I know you're struggling a little." He knows me too well. He starts looking through my closet, and comes across this royal blue, fitted midi dress I bought last year but never wore. He takes it out and puts it on the bed. "You need to bring this."

"Isn't it like, super cold there? When would I even get the chance to wear it?" I'm just being realistic here.

"It's not cold inside restaurants or bars. Just bring it, what if you end up going on a date?" He winks.

"I am pretty sure the chances of that happening are exponentially low."

17

"Speaking of dates, have you groomed your jungle?"

Is he for real right now? "What do you mean?" I know exactly what he means, but I want to know what he has to say.

"You know, the BUSH." He looks down to my crotch.

"JACE! It is always groomed, what the heck." It's true, my mother has put this fear in my head since I started puberty that if I am not as smooth as a baby, it's a sin. So, I allow my pubic hair to be ripped every other month by a total stranger.

"Okay, okay. Just making sure. I mean you have been looking pretty homeless these past few weeks, and you never know, when in Korea..." He gives me another wink.

"Jace! Who do you think I am? I haven't slept with any of the guys I do know, you really think I'll just sleep with some random person I barely know...WHO LIVES IN A DIFFERENT CONTINENT?"

"All I'm saying is never say never."

"Yeah, okay. I'll be on the lookout for anyone who is willing to sleep with me." I say sarcastically. I've never been promiscuous. Nothing wrong with it at all, I love it when women embrace their sexuality. I've just always been one who has always been afraid of the whole ordeal of sleeping around because I just don't trust people.

After I thoroughly over pack my suitcase, Jace and I head to the kitchen to make some dinner.

"Chicken salad?" He asks.

"Yeah, let's do that."

"How are you feeling? Still a bit nervous?" He rubs my back while he's warming up the chicken.

"Honestly, Jace. I think I might be more excited than nervous. I mean, I'm still scared about how we can pull this off without my parents finding out, but is it bad that I don't care?" I felt so bad saying that. My parents are so trusting of me. I do feel guilty that I'm going behind their backs and lying to them. "I just feel like, if my parents didn't care about the opinions of

18

our community, I'd be more open to telling them the truth about everything in my life. It's almost as I've been forced to live this double life, consistently struggling with both my American and Pakistani identities. Going on a trip with your best friend isn't exactly a big deal in western culture. But, being Pakistani and a girl...going on a trip with you can easily become a disgusting rumor. It's not like Pakistani kids have any desires, wants, or needs. God forbid we have a little fun!" I pause to take a deep breath. "But, regardless...the guilt is still there, no matter how much logic I try to feed myself."

"I know you're feeling guilty right now. I can sense it off of you, trust me. Just think about it this way...when you're all grey and wrinkly, and your labias are hanging to the floor, at that point you won't be worrying about your parents. You'll be cherishing the fond memories you made by being a little disobedient. You don't want to live your life by 'what if's'."

He's actually right, yet again. Maybe I should be listening to him more often.

We start getting ready for bed. We decided to sleep in one room tonight because we were too excited to stop planning. Our flight leaves early in the morning, around seven from LAX. We start checking off what we need.

"Wallets?" I ask.

"Check!" Jace replies.

"Passports?"

"Check!"

"Itinerary?"

"Check!" He looked down at our itinerary that he made and printed out. "Oh...also," he looks back up at me and tries to mutter something but I can't hear him. "We might be going to a concert."

A concert? "Jace, why don't you ask me before you make a decision?"

"I feel like you would have said no." He's right about that.

"I'm not boring, you know! I'm quite flexible. You just make impulsive decisions, to which I question your choices. Anyways, what concert?"

"So, NOWus are playing the day before we leave and I already bought the tickets so you have to go."

"You know what, I'm not even mad."

"You aren't?" He asks.

"Yeah, I'm not. I'm just kinda going with the flow, you know? Who knows, it might be fun, although I don't know any of their songs."

"Zara, I swear you'll love it. Their concerts are so lively. The leader of the group, AJ, is just full of energy." He looks away into the distance as if he's daydreaming.

"I believe you. I think that'd be the best way to end the trip. A bit cliche, but I think I'm okay with that."

We both get into bed, and I take some melatonin pills to knock me out or else I'll have another sleepless night from all my thoughts.

Jace gets up abruptly, and turns to me. "Shit, we forgot one more thing!"

"What are we missing?" I ask.

He yells out, "Condoms!" and throws a bunch of them on me.

"Oh, God! Take the gloves of the devil away from me!" I laugh, as I swat them off of me.

"Goodnight, you nasty swine." Jace kisses my forehead.

"Goodnight, devil's assistant." I immediately shut my eyes. My nerves have gone away, and I'm starting to feel more and more excited about this trip. I finally have something to look forward to.

CHAPTER THREE

The Arrival

I wake to a pillow smacking my face. "Wake up! We're late!" Jace shouts. Sleepily I lie there for a brief moment, trying to comprehend what he is talking about. After a few seconds, I scream and jump off of bed once I realize we had overslept.

"How did this happen?! I swear I set an alarm clock!" Panicked, I check my phone to see if I did in fact set an alarm, but I didn't! My hands can't stop shaking and I feel as if my legs have completely stopped working.

"It doesn't matter, stop wasting time, just start moving!" Jace grabs his luggage while still wearing pjs and stacks it by the door. "Honestly, just come out in your pjs. No one will care!"

I don't argue, and quickly grab my luggage. We order an Uber, and head to LAX. The LA traffic adds more to my anxiety. We literally are five minutes away from the airport but with traffic, the GPS says fifteen. Our flight takes off in thirty!

I start to panic. "We aren't going to make it, Jace. This is what happens when you lie to your parents. This is a sign we shouldn't have done this!"

"We will be fine! Be positive. You're stressing me the hell out!"

Looking over, I can see he's equally stressed out, I just seem to be the one actually showing it.

We start running to security check, and sprint all the way to our gate with just minutes till the flight takes off! I felt as if I were in the Home Alone movie when Kevin Mcallister's family is running to their gate. I don't remember the last time I ran this fast. Even Jace is struggling to catch his breath.

Spotting the plane boarding, Jace starts to slow down but obviously, I don't get the memo. I run directly into him, and we both fall in a heap in front of the flight attendant.

"Are you guys okay?" The flight attendant looks at us - trying her best not to laugh - as we lay on top of one another.

"Yeah, we were just afraid we were going to miss our flight." Jace helps me up and shoulders his bag.

"You made it in time, we were just about to close the gate." The flight attendant checks our passports and boarding passes. "Enjoy your flight!"

We navigate the narrow aisle to our seats. As soon as I sit down, a gust of cold air from the vent leaves goosebumps all over my body. "Great, I'm gonna die from hypothermia before I reach South Korea." I complain to Jace.

He twists it closed. "No, you won't. Actually, you might. You barely have any meat on your bones. Lemme ask if they have a body bag around here. My new year's resolution is not to procrastinate anymore." He laughs and I elbow him hard. "Ouch!"

Now I'm laughing.

Please fasten your seatbelts, we are about to take off." The flight attendant makes the announcement as she walks through the cabin. The plane moves and I begin reciting the prayers my mom taught me for protection.

"Really? You're reciting your prayers to Allah for protection, while you lied to your parents?" Jace chuckles. "Allah ain't gonna protect a sinner."

Eyes closed, I continue to recite them while he makes fun of me. "Well, that's between me and God. Don't forget we are on this plane because of you."

"Touche." He replies.

After watching Interstellar, I decided to take a nap, which lasted for a hour until Jace woke me up.

"Hey, you awake?" He nudged me.

"Am now." I take my time opening up my eyes. My back is killing me from sleeping in such a weird position. I can't wait till we get to our hotel and I can sleep on a proper bed.

"I kinda wanted to tell you something." His expression is serious, something I don't see quite often.

"What's up?" I sit up straight, alert now.

He pauses and looks down. "So, the night we got drunk and you bought the tickets...that was actually me. I may have used your credit card and laptop to make it seem as if you were on board with the plan, but it was all me. You were knocked out in the corner."

I'm in shock. Jace definitely is more spontaneous than I am and makes impulsive decisions, but not to this extent.

"Why didn't you just tell me?" I ask.

"When I remembered what had happened that night, I got really scared. And seeing how you freaked out...well, it became more of a reason not to tell you."

"Okay, I can see that." He's right, I would have gotten more mad if he had told me then.

"Honestly, Zara, I know I do some crazy things at times," a complete understatement, "and I seem as if I have no care in the world..." he pauses and takes a deep breath. "But, I've been extremely exhausted since medical school started. Both mentally and physically."

Wow, I've never heard him say anything along those lines before.

"But you seemed fine?" He genuinely did, so I'm surprised to hear all this.

"Yeah, I did. I just didn't want to show it. I don't like showing when I'm incredibly upset or stressed out because you go out of your way to make sure I'm okay. I just didn't want to burden you."

My heart just sank hearing that.

"Jace," I grab his hand. "We met for a reason. I stayed friends with you because you were the first person in my life to really listen to me. You were the first person I really opened up to. I think you feel the same way about me, right?"

"Yeah, of course." He smiles and tightens his hand around mine.

"You can never be a burden to me. Ever. Your worries are mine. Your problems are mine. You're my best friend, and it upsets me to know that you feel like you couldn't talk to me about any of this. Of course I'm going to go out of my way to make sure you're okay, idiot. You'd do the same for me. That's what family does. We look out for each other. What's been stressing you out?"

"I know you feel the same way. It's just...we have to consistently study so much! It's taking a toll on me. I mean, I'm not complaining, I'm VERY blessed to have gotten into medical school. I just realized I haven't really lived. Like, during undergrad, we barely went out. We just studied, or watched movies during our free time. That was fun, don't get me wrong, but I think we didn't take advantage of how much time we had and what we could have done."

"No, I completely understand. I agree, I feel like I didn't do anything as fun because I was always scared of my parents finding out. I think that prevented me from experimenting and trying new things and now...I kind of regret it."

Jace nods. "I know. I think I felt guilty for having a little fun because that would mean I'm letting my family down. Being a first generation college graduate in my family, there's always been an immense amount of pressure to do well in school and set a good example for my siblings. I guess this didn't allow me to make mistakes, or think for myself. It prevented me from doing things I wanted to do because I was just thin-

24

king for my family. Now, that I'm in medical school, I realize I don't have time for myself, yet again."

"I don't think I've ever heard you open up like this before. This probably has been bothering you for a while, huh?"

"Yeah, it has been. Like, during undergrad, I feel as though school wasn't as intense for us as it is now. We are running out of time to do the things we want to do. I mean, we've been saying we will plan a trip here or there, but never actually do it."

"You're actually right. The only trip we've ever made was to In n Out and back to the library."

"Exactly." We both laugh.

I sigh. "I feel that pressure, too. For me, it was about how my actions would reflect on my family. The fear of disappointing my parents became a motivation in itself. The culture that I come from, it very much stresses on the idea of collectivism. Like, let's say I got super drunk, and someone in the community found out. They'll spread rumors and gossip. That would make my parents look REALLY bad. Dad's a professor, too, so I have to keep our image even more clean. At the end, my family and I would have the badge of not being from a respectable family just from that one action. Plus, I'm a girl. Somehow girls always suffer through more consequences than boys. My actions can either raise their heads up high with pride, or down out of shame. I think that's why I didn't do anything that was considered wild. It's just stupid! Drinking, having sex...why are these considered as vices! They don't make you a bad person in my eyes, just as long as you don't hurt someone and are responsible about it. Right?!"

"I totally agree, you're right."

"I know I am!" I get more aggressively emotional. " I refuse to believe that the all merciful God we believe in weighs things like this more than being a good person. I see so many religious people in my extended family and community who have great attendance at the mosque, pray five times a day, but man...they've betrayed people, talked behind their backs and hurt them without fearing God. But, when it comes to drinking, having sex or anything else that is considered sinful, they are quick to say 'fear Allah'! Like, don't bring God into this! The hypocrisy just blows my mind."

I didn't realize how emotional I was getting until I knocked over my cup of water off of the tray table. It splashed the person across the aisle who glared at me.

"Okay, relax, Malala. Everyone can hear you." Jace whispers out of embarrassment.

"Alright, I'm relaxed. But you get what I'm saying, right?"

"Yes, and so do the people in front and behind us."

"It's just, this talk made me realize how much we have been living for other people besides us. Why are we constantly worrying about what others will say? We haven't been fair to ourselves. We worked hard, but didn't play hard. We neglected romance, our desires, curiosity, and for what?!" I felt as if I was making a speech before a battle. "Enough is enough. On this trip we need to make a few rules for ourselves."

Jace's eyes light up. "I'm on board, captain! Let's hear it."

"First, we cannot complain. Well, that goes more for me because I can be a wimp."

"True." He nods.

"Second, we can't be afraid of trying new things."

"Okay, I like where this is going."

"And third..."

Jace interrupts before I say anything," We have sex with as many people as possible. I'm thinking we take on the whole city to compensate for not sleeping around too much."

"Um, I'm not trying to get an STD, sorry." I roll my eyes as we both laugh.

"Okay, I'll come up with a new rule. We have to be spontaneous and for the first time, not think about others. Just live in the movement."

"I won't argue with that one. Just gotta make sure we don't spontaneously do something illegal and end up in a foreign prison. Now THAT will bring shame to my family."

"Yeah, okay we won't do anything that's TOO illegal." He winks. Jesus, he winks way too much.

"I'm really excited, Jace. I feel like I'm in this coming-of-age movie but like in our mid twenties."

"Yeah, it feels that way. More for you than me. Some of us have actually gone through puberty."

I couldn't help it, I laughed so loud, and may have woken up a few people around us from the dirty looks I got. "I just don't wanna be that weirdo that never takes a sip from her drink during a game of 'Never Have I Ever'. That was so embarrassing during welcome week; I felt like everyone in my class judged me as some loser who never did anything remotely exciting. I'm not that person. I'm fun, damn it!" Pouting, I shook the last few crumbs from my pretzel bag into my mouth.

"If someone has to say that they're fun, they're probably not as fun as you think."

"Whatever. Okay, but I am fun. You know it. Say it!"

"Yes, okay you are somewhat fun." He flashes a smile.

"Screw the shame I was taught to feel for not conforming to the societal norms of being a desi girl! For the next week, I'm living out my teenage dream that I never got to."

CHAPTER FOUR

Lost and Found

"Excuse me, Ma'm," I feel a hand on my shoulder. "Could you please put your seat upright, we are about to land." The flight attendant gestures to my seat. I look over and see Jace is still asleep. Gosh, how long was I asleep for?

"Hey, wake up." I shake him up gently.

"What happened, where am I?"

"Um, we are landing right now."

"Oh okay. Did you just wake up, too?"

"Yeah, the flight attendant woke me up."

"How long were we knocked out for?"

"Oh, man. I don't know. We've been sleeping for about eight hours I believe."

"Eight hours?! I feel like that's the most we have slept in one night."

"Wow, you're right. I don't think I've slept more than five hours a night since grad school started. No wonder I feel like a new person."

"You feel refreshed, huh?" He asks.

"Oh yeah, I could literally go for a run right now, I have so much energy."

"Okay, calm down there, Usain Bolt," he jokes. "Let's land first, and then you can run as much as you want...hopefully after men."

The captain turns on the fasten seatbelt sign as we begin to land. As the wheels hit the ground, we feel a huge jolt but it was quite a smooth landing otherwise.

"Hello, everyone. This is your captain speaking. We have landed at Incheon International Airport. It is about three o'clock in the afternoon. The weather is around forty degrees Fahrenheit. Welcome to Seoul, South Korea and I hope you enjoy your stay."

We wait around for people to grab their bags from the overhead bin. I'd rather wait till the plane empties before I grab my stuff, otherwise I just feel rushed. We make our way to baggage claim. "My back is hurting like crazy." I turn to Jace as I put my hand behind my back rubbing it a little.

"You know what helps to relieve back pain?"

"What?" I ask thinking he's going to give some helpful medical advice.

"Sex!"

I roll my eyes as he says that. "Your mind is always in the gutter."

"Well, maybe yours should be too. Maybe then you'd catch something on that web downstairs."

I sometimes question how we became friends. He points to a Toy Story suitcase. "Is that yours?"

"Ha, ha. Very funny." I was about to roll my eyes and stopped. I realize something that I forgot to ask him. "I never asked...where are we staying? You took care of our hotel, right?"

He didn't look me in the eyes but replied back with a simple yes.

"Okay, where is it?" I ask.

"Don't worry about it. It's somewhere fun, I promise. Relax! Remember what we said on the plane." Shit, he's right.

We grab our suitcases and head to the front desk to ask where we can get a taxi. They order a taxi for us and tell us to go outside. We step out and it hits us. We. Are. In. South. Korea. I begin to get butterflies in my stomach. It's really, really cold compared to California. My jaw seems to be frozen shut, even though we've been standing outside for only a few seconds.

Jace looks out in the distance and says, "Are we Godzilla, because we are about to destroy this city." We both laugh.

"I don't think we will be destroying anything in these clothes." We look down at what we're wearing and realize we are still in our pjs.

Jace looks back up, "Oh, look. Our taxi is here."

"Hello!" I greet our driver as I get in.

"Hello, hello!" He's a really friendly old gentleman with the most welcoming smile ever. Jace shows him the itinerary with the address to our hotel. We start driving through the traffic. There are cars coming from left to right. I'm still in disbelief that I am in a completely different continent than my parents right now. Speaking of parents, I realized mine never called me.

"Jace, my parents never called me."

"That's a good thing, right?" He questions.

"You think I should call them? To make it less suspicious?"

"Uhh.." Jace doesn't have an answer.

"I'll call them through my Facebook, and say I'm calling them through the app because the signal at our apartment is being funky."

Jace looks at me with amazement. "Wow, I've created a professional liar. I'm so proud." He wipes a fake tear away. "Just call them once we get to our hotel."

Honestly, I don't even want to worry about that right now. I'm just in awe of Korea. Actually, I'm more in awe of how we managed to pull this whole thing off. I pause to look around the places we are driving by and take it all in. The streets are clean but a little congested. There are tall buildings on either side of us. There are K-Pop posters everywhere! I see Jace starting to get excited once he sees them. The closer we get

30

to our designated hotel, the more and more K-Pop posters I start noticing.

"Wow, they really are about that K-Pop life."

"Yeah…" His tone just gives off that vibe that he's hiding something.

"Why does it feel like you're hiding something from me?"

"I'm not." He responds quickly, like a child responding to a parent when caught doing something wrong.

"Spill, I know you're hiding something and I wanna hear it from that dirty little mouth of yours," I whisper because I don't want the elderly gentleman to think my friend is an idiot.

"Well…the reason you are seeing an abundance of posters relating to K-Pop may have something to do with the fact that we are in the hub of all of the K-Pop productions studios."

I pause and think how I should react to this. Should I be angry because now I know that most of the time will consist of him stalking K-Pop groups, like a lion stalks his prey…or should I just go along with it?

"I don't know what you're thinking, and it is starting to make me nervous."

"I'm not even mad." I reply.

He looks at me with disbelief. "Okay, now you're really starting to scare me. Where is my overthinking, neurotic best friend and what have you done with her?!"

I laugh, "I swear I'm not mad. Just promise me we won't be K-Pop hunting the whole time."

"I cross my heart and hope to die." He's so dramatic.

After about an hour, we reached our hotel. He wasn't lying, it is very close to all the production companies. We head inside the hotel and Jace checks us in.

"I asked for the top floor so we can have the best view." He grins as we cross the lobby. Jace tends to go all out.

We get inside the elevator, and are surrounded by beautiful people. I can't help but notice how glass-like their skin is. I wish I could just straight up ask for their skincare routine, but that might be a little weird considering we are still in our pjs and could definitely use a shower. One of the girls may have turned the other way once she got a whiff of us.

The elevator door opens to our floor, and we start walking to our room. "After you, milady." Jace bows down as the door swings open.

There's a closet as soon as we walk in, so we set our luggage inside before exploring. A living room sits separate from the bedroom. Both have large windows all around, allowing the sunlight to stream in and Jace was right...the view is amazing. The decor is all maroon, while the couches and bed sheets are white. The bathroom has white marble countertops and flooring. Everything looks amazing.

"We're in Korea, baby!" Jace shrieks.

"South. South Korea." Absently, I correct him. He's probably sick and tired of me correcting him by now.

Jace completely ignores me, yet again, and heads towards the bathroom. His voice is muffled through the closed door. "We should start getting ready. It's almost five. I think we definitely need a shower, especially from the looks we were getting in the elevator. We can look all cute and head to one of the cafes nearby. I put the name of it on the itinerary."

I head to the closet and grab my larger suitcase while Jace is in the shower. I start pulling out some of my clothes. The first thing I see is my grey NASA shirt. It seems like a trendy thing to wear. I grab that, a black scarf and thermal tights to wear under my jeans. My legs were shivering when we got out of the airport. I feel like we didn't properly pack for this weather- a downfall of being a Californian.

Jace comes out after he showers and looks at the clothes I laid out on the bed. "You know we are on vacation, right?" He gives me a judgmental look.

"Uh, yeah?"

"Okay, so why are we wearing clothes that practically says 'I'm a twelve year old boy, come kidnap me'?"

"What do you mean?! This is trendy!" I defend myself.

"Alright, you know what, do you, boo. I ain't saying nothing." He throws his hands up in defeat.

"Thank you, I appreciate that." I walk away and towards the bathroom.

Jace knocks on the bathroom door after about ten minutes. "Hurry up! The city awaits."

"Okay, coming out!" I may have dozed off in the shower once the hot water hit me. It was defrosting my frozen bones. Getting out of the shower, I dry myself off. I brought my brush blow dryer that gives the perfect blowout, and after learning how to do it from beauty gurus on YouTube, I'm quite proud of myself. After about ten minutes, my arms are tired but thankfully I'm done. I move onto makeup. Do I feel daring? Should I try a winged eyeliner?! I gather the courage to grab my liquid liner, and begin drawing. I try to remember those makeup videos I watched. As I'm about to flick the wing, Jace pounds on the bathroom door.

"What is taking so long?!" He yells.

"I'm doing a wing!" I yell back.

"A what? Who?!" Gosh, he can be so annoying.

I open the door, and let him in. "I was this close to messing up my winged eyeliner!"

"Oh, you meant wing. I thought there was like some imaginary person inside that you were referring to. Wow, it actually looks good."

"Really?" I'm surprised.

"Yeah, if a ten year old were doing it." He bursts out laughing.

"Okay, now that you've made me feel all self conscious, help me." I hold out the tube.

"I got you baby girl, I was just kidding. You did a very good job. I'm just gonna grab a q tip and just fix the edges on both sides." He licks the top of the q tip, and sharpens the edges.

Once he's done, I apply mascara on my lashes and conce-aler under my eyes and around my nose. I top it off with a nude pink lipstick, with a bit of chapstick on top. I reach out to grab some blush, but it seems as though some color has come back to my cheeks - a sight I haven't seen in a while. Lastly, I spritz on some Marc Jacobs perfume.

"Damn, you look good." Jace checks me out. "At least the makeup does, the outfit could use a bit of work."

I roll my eyes. "We don't have time to 'Queer Eye' me right now. Let's go, I'm in desperate need of a hot chocolate and some food."

We go back into the living room where our stuff is. I grab my small, black Longchamp and stuff it with my wallet, the itinerary, phone, chapstick, and gum. I see Jace grabbing something from his bag, and putting it inside mine.

"What did you put in there?" I ask.

"Oh, some money, in case we need it."

"Oh, okay." I grab my scarf, jacket, quickly put on my black Converse and run to Jace who is by the door already.

"We should take a picture to commemorate our first day here!" Jace takes out his phone and we snap a quick picture. We then make our way to the elevator, and down to the lobby.

"Okay, so I printed out a map. This will help us guide our-selves." Jace gives me the map and I start following him out-side. We are slapped with a gust of cold breeze. "Oh my God! Did frosty just slap me with his dick?! Because I'm freezing'!" Jace shouts.

I laugh. "You're right. I feel like I just motorboated Elsa!" Jace turns to me, and we both burst out in laughter.

"I was NOT expecting you to say that. Who are you?!" Jace grabs my arm and gives me a hug. We continue walking aimlessly, but I think we are heading the right way because I start to see the posters that we passed by near one of the production studios. Out in the distance, I see a homeless man sitting on the side of the sidewalk. I stop for a second to look through my purse for some money. As I am rummaging through the disaster that is the inside of my bag, Jace bolts off yelling, "THERE'S GOT7, OH MY GOD!"

I look up to see him running across the street like a paparazzi photographer. "Jace, what are you doing?!" I run after him, but he's already too far from me and gets lost in the sea of fans. I look around to see if I can find him, but he's nowhere to be found. Hyperventilating, I grab my phone, and dial his number. He doesn't answer. I start to think I'm going to be stranded out here in the streets with the homeless man I saw. Thankfully, before making future plans for my residence on the streets, Jace texts asking to meet up in the cafe that is on the itinerary.

"Oh, thank God." I let out a sigh of relief. I take out the itinerary and begin looking for the cafe's name, one that I cannot pronounce. I start walking, trying to look for any signs of this cafe. I want to stop a passerby and ask for directions, but I'm just afraid that I won't be able to communicate. Thankfully, I find a store around the corner with a poster of Justin Bieber on it's window. There are a group of people standing outside of it. I ask one of the girls standing in front if she was in line, and she gestures to the store. I'm assuming she didn't speak English and I can just walk inside. I open the door and find the cashier sitting on a stool on the left hand side.

"Uh, hello? Do you speak English?" I ask. He gives me a blank stare. "Um, do you know where this cafe is?" I point at the name on the itinerary. He still gives me no answer and right about now, I'm this close to shitting my pants. I'm going to kill Jace when I see him. Before the waterworks begin, I hear a deep, low angelic voice, one who spoke English with an Australian accent.

"Hi, can we help you?" I turn around to see two Korean men standing behind me. I was surprised that the voice came out of the tiny blonde one. Standing next to him is a taller brunette, with short hair and broad shoulders. They look like they had just stepped out of a magazine. They seemed to be wearing a touch of eyeshadow, accentuating their eyes. I'm not judging, it added to their already gorgeous features. Hell, they pull it off better than I ever could. They are dressed up in very trendy clothes, putting my NASA shirt to shame.

"Yes! Yes, you can." I think they sensed the desperation in my voice from earlier. I probably sound like I just escaped a kidnapping. " I lost my best friend. This idiot ran off while I was going through my purse, leaving me alone for some dumb band called got milk, or something like that." I see them chuckle, but I continue to word vomit. "I've been walking around trying to find this cafe and then I started getting these weird thoughts that I may have lost him forever, and I'll be stuck in Korea, living on the streets and eating birds like a savage." I finally stop talking hysterically, take a few breaths and look up to see them laughing. Oh God, I've made a fool out of myself.

"Wow, it seems like you had quite a day!" The blonde one comforts me, but with a touch of laughter. The brunette seems to be a little shy.

"Yeah, you could say that." I laugh nervously.

"What's the cafe called?" The blonde one asks.

"Uh, I can't pronounce it but it's this one." I hand over the itinerary. I look outside to see that the group of people are still there. "Why are there so many people waiting in line? That is a line, right?" I ask.

The brunette speaks up, who also happens to have an Australian accent but less of a deep voice. It's more soothing, like listening to the waves crashing on the shore. "Oh they're waiting for..." He gets interrupted by the blonde one.

"They're waiting to spot some K-Pop stars. They tend to come by this store quite often."

"Oh, that sucks for them...the K-Pop stars, I mean. I feel bad...it seems like they don't get much privacy."

They both exchange blank looks and then look back at the itinerary. "Oh, this is like a ten minute walk. It's not far." The blonde one glances over at the brunette. "My friend can take you there." The brunette immediately looks at him with confusion. I see the blonde one nudging him.

"Yeah, no problem. I can take you there." He hesitantly offers.

"Oh, no, it's okay. I'll manage to find my way, can you just give me the directions?" I start feeling really bad.

"No, honestly. It's not a problem at all." He shines a comforting smile.

"Thank you so much!" I am so relieved. I honestly was getting worried thinking about getting lost again.

"You two can go through the back door, it's a shortcut to where the cafe is." The blonde points to the back.

"Thank you so, so much. I'll never forget this!" I leap out to hug him, something I normally wouldn't do because that's invasion of personal space, but he doesn't understand how badly I was suffering.

"No worries at all!" He hugs back. "Have fun!"

"I will!" I look at the brunette and start following him. I turn back to see the blonde one smiling and waving at me as walks out through the front door.

We step outside and for some weird reason, I turn right.

"Oh, we have to make a left." He smiles. He's equally as nervous as me. I didn't notice before, he has the deepest dimples I have ever seen.

"My bad, I clearly don't know my way around here."

"No problem. Where are you visiting from?" He asks.

"Los Angeles. This is kind of a very, very spontaneous trip for my best friend and me. How about you? I'm assuming you're visiting from Australia?"

"I am from Australia, but I'm not visiting. I actually live here."

Live here? Why is he living here? "Oh, do you work here or something?"

"Yeah, I live here for work. I've actually been living here for a couple years now."

"Does your family live here as well?" I don't mean to pry, but I want to know.

"No, they live in Australia. I visit when I can, but... with work it can be quite hard." He looks down at his feet. I can tell he got a bit sad saying that. He quickly changes the topic. "I really like your shirt. Do you like NASA?"

I had completely forgotten about what I was wearing. Shit, I hope he doesn't think I'm one of those space freaks...which I kind of am. "Yes, I do. I actually am a total space geek. You can ask me anything about space, from Einstein's relativity to quantum physics to how many moons Saturn has."

"Wow, smart girl." His eyes crinkle as he smiles. I get butterflies. I need to murder them right now. I'm not about to have butterflies for someone I just met half a second ago.

"I'm not that smart." I titter. The amount of shyness that is being exchanged between us is astronomical.

"You seem like you are. I also am very much of a space geek as well. I literally just watched a quick episode of Ancient Aliens before coming to the store."

I pause and look at him as if HE is some sort of alien being. "You're kidding me?! I love that show! I watch it all the time, and even force my best friend to watch it with me but he's not really into it...or anyone that I know of."

"Your best friend...he sounds like an interesting character."

"Oh, you have no idea! He is something else. But, I wouldn't have it any other way. I mean, right now, I want to murder him and make a cold case episode out of it, if you know what I mean." I laugh.

"Wait." He stops walking. "Before we go any further, I have to know. You're not a serial killer, are you?" He doesn't smile, so I start to freak out thinking that he might actually think I'm somewhat of a Ted Bundy character.

"No! No! I swear, I'm not. Jesus, do I give off that vibe?" I freak out.

"No, I'm joking!" He bursts into laughter. Damn, his accent is so charming and I can't help but blush.

We pass the homeless man again, and I stop. "Wait here, don't run off. I just gotta do something real quick." I can see the confusion on his face.

"Uh, yeah, okay."

Quickly I run to the homeless man and hand him some money and make my way back.

"That was really sweet of you."

"Oh, it's nothing. I was in the middle of giving him some money, and that's when my best friend took off to see got milk, or whatever, so I never got the chance to."

"You're full of surprises, aren't you?" He smiles with his eyes. I find his shyness quite cute. Is he trying to flirt with me? No, he couldn't be. I brush it off with a nervous giggle. "You're not into K-Pop, are you?" He asks.

"Geez, what gave it away?" I try to be subtle with my sarcasm.

"Got milk? The band is actually called GOT7." He chuckles.

"Ah, that makes more sense. Yeah, I'm not super into K-Pop, but my best friend is." We continue to walk. There's this awkward silence between us. We both speak at the same time and then laugh.

"What were you going to say?" I ask.

"I was going to ask you..uhh, about the weather." He replies.

I have an inkling that's not what he was going to ask. "I feel like you were about to ask something else." Now I'm grinning. Wait, am I flirting?!

"Were YOU about to say something?" He asks me.

His eyes were so distracting, I forgot what I was about to say, honestly. "I actually don't remember. I was trying to fill in the silence."

"Well, you don't have to. We're here." He points at the cafe. We are standing right outside of it.

"Oh, that went by fast." I am surprised how quickly ten minutes went by.

"Yeah, it did. Didn't it?" He replies back. We look at each other with this discomfort of knowing that we are about to say goodbye. "So, this is goodbye, huh?" He scratches his head.

"Yeah...I guess so." I nervously laugh. "Thank you so much. You have no idea how much trouble you saved me."

"It was my pleasure, honestly." We both are staring at each other. He hesitantly turns around and starts walking away. I begin to feel sad seeing him walk away from me. Why do I get this urge to stop him? I hear Jace's voice in my head with something along the lines of me growing a pair of ovaries, and to run after him. I hesitate, but this can't be the last time I see him.

I find myself walking towards him and yell out, "Hey!" I instantly regret saying it. He turns around. I have no idea what's about to come out of my mouth, but I walk over to him. "I don't normally do this, but I don't know why I got so sad knowing that I'll never see you again. I know, this is crazy." I look at my hands out of embarrassment. "But, I'm doing this thing on this trip where I live in the moment. So, here I am. Living in the moment."

He smiles while he looks at me. "I'm really glad you stopped me. I was quite sad to walk away from you if I'm being honest." I felt so much relief knowing I wasn't the only one feeling this way, but also surprised it was being reciprocated. It gave me the courage to do the next thing.

"Would you like to grab drinks later?" I ask very shyly. "I know it's last minute and you can totally say..."

He immediately answers with, "I'd love to."

"Wow, okay." I smile, not being able to hide my joy. I cannot wait to tell Jace, he's going to be so proud of me...after I kill him. I give him the information of the hotel from the itinerary and we agree to meet at the hotel bar around eight o'clock. "So, I'll see you later."

"Yeah, can't wait." His smile matches mine. He turns around and starts walking away. I turn around to face the cafe's door, only to see Jace frozen in place, sitting at a table. Was he watching me the whole time?

I break out of my trance and walk inside, ready to kill him. "DID YOU SERIOUSLY ABANDON ME, ON THE STREETS?! I thought I was going to die out here all alone, and I was also scared that you would be killed by hooligans." Jace says nothing. It looks like he just saw a ghost. "Are you just going to sit there with that stupid, dumb, idiotic look on your face, or are you going to say something?!" I yell.

"Do you know..."

I interrupt, "Oh, if you're about to say something smartasslike, save it! I've had it with your..." He places his hand over my mouth.

"DO YOU KNOW WHO THAT WAS?! THE PERSON YOU WERE TALKING TO?!" He's acting so maniacally.

I move his hand away, completely changing my demeanor. "Oh, yeah! I just asked him out! I was going to tell you after my little angry rant, but then I saw your face and I forgot about that. He's the one who helped me find this cafe."

"Do you know who he is?!"

"Oh, I actually didn't get his name." How did I not ask his name? Wait, I didn't even tell him my name!

"Bitch, that was AJ. AJ!" He goes into a complete frenzy mode. AJ? I had to stop and think about it for a second. Where have I heard this name before? Wait. Then it hit me like a truck. That was AJ from NOWus.

CHAPTER FIVE

The Date

I'm engulfed with shock. This time, I'm frozen in place in my seat instead of Jace. Every single word we exchanged starts to replay in my head. I freaked out in front of him and made myself look like a total idiot! God, I even said that I'd have to eat birds if I got stranded! Who says that?! He almost saw me cry like a little child! I look back and cringe at my failed flirting.

"Oh, God! I'm such a freak! I totally made myself sound like a neurotic, serial killer in front of him!" I plant my hands in my face.

"You have to tell me everything! I'm sure it wasn't that bad." Jace comforts me.

"I said I wanted to make a cold case file out of you."

His eyes wander to the corner of the cafe, as if he's trying to picture me saying that and shudders. "Yeah, that does make you sound like a serial killer." He pauses and pats me on the head. "A SEXY serial killer." As if that would make me feel any better.

"Jesus, I called GOT7, got milk. Oh, and get this. I said I wasn't into K-Pop."

Jace places his fingers on his templates and says, "Ay Dios mio, what am I going to do with you?!"

"Maybe help me get ready for my date? Which, by the way, he said yes to!" Jace's face lights up.

"Oh yeah! You asked him out?! I cannot believe it. You have never asked out a mortal, let alone a K-Pop star! I don't think I've ever been more proud of you." He grabs my arm, brings me closer to him in a very tight embrace. I felt as if my rib cages were going to crack.

"Ah!" I ache in pain. "I'd like to make it to my date, please. With all my bones intact."

He loosens his grip. "Alright, let's head out now. I also got you this sandwich and the hot chocolate you wanted."

"Thank you, I didn't realize how hungry I was during this whole ordeal." I grab the sandwich and attempt to take a bite out of it, but Jace takes it from me.

"What are you doing? There's no time to eat right now. Let's go and tell me everything as we walk!" He grabs my arm, not realizing he's squeezing it so tightly. He's walking so fast, it feels as if I'm flying.

As soon as we reach our room, I open my suitcase and start throwing clothes on the floor. I try on some of the blouses I brought with me, but I feel like they're not good enough. What does one wear on a date with a K-Pop star?!

"I have nothing to wear!" I throw my hands up in frustration. I sit on the bed thinking this is a terrible idea. I let out a sigh. "I don't think I'm good enough. I don't feel like I am."

Jace walks over and places his arm around me. "Don't say that. Don't you dare say that again, okay?" He puts his hand under my chin and lifts my face. "You're absolutely beautiful. On top of that, you're so smart and interesting. Believe me, if anything he's not good enough. You're a catch, and if he doesn't catch you, I will!" I blush hearing his little pep talk. "Okay, I'm going to see what we can do. There has to be something in that suitcase that we can work with." We look through my clothes. After a couple minutes, something catches both of our eyes.

"I completely forgot you made me pack this blue midi dress!" For the first time ever, I think I'm happy to see a dress in my vicinity. "Jace, I will never not listen to you again!" I leap onto him as if I just won a battle.

"Aren't you glad I made you put away the rest of the NASA shirts?"

"Very, very much. Thank you." I wear the dress and I actually don't look that bad. In fact, I felt a little confident and as what I envisioned a twenty-five year old should possess when I was younger. This dress accentuates my semi curves a lot more. " I think I can work with this." I check myself out in the mirror.

"Really? I thought you hated fitted dresses."

"Yeah, I do...but considering how I'm trying new things, why not add this to the mix?" I wink at him.

"Who are you?!" He gapes at me with profound amazement.

"Just someone who's going on a date with a K-Pop star." I shrug.

"I'm loving this new confidence. Why couldn't this happen years ago? Or even a few minutes ago?!"

"Well, it's happening right this second." I skip over to my suitcase. "Oh, and I also packed these black heels. The heel is tiny, so there's a low chance of me tripping and dying right in front of him."

"You packed heels? When?" He asks while I take them out.

"Uh, when you put this dress into my bag. I figured I should add in something that would work well with it."

"That was actually really good thinking. I'm actually looking back at that moment when you complained about this dress. I said that you can wear this on a date. Do you remember what you said?"

"Uh, I think I said something like the chances of that happening are low?"

"Yes, you said that. Now look how the tables have turned. Not only are you going on a date, but it's with my dream guy. But hey, I ain't mad." He laughs. "It's about time you get some vitamin D and that's coming from a future doctor."

"The only way I'll be getting vitamin D is through sunlight and food...and that's coming from a future PA. Plus, I only exchanged a few words with him. Hell, he doesn't even know my name!"

"You don't need to know names to get some...vitamin D, if you know what I mean." He winks.

I ignore him and head to the bathroom. Thankfully, my hair still looks good from the blowout I gave myself. I wash my face to take off the makeup from earlier and apply some moisturizer, letting it set for a few seconds. I may have gone overboard with it because I wanted to give myself that dewy glow. Now, it just looks like I've been sweating like a pig. I realize it's not setting in, so I wipe some of it off, grab my makeup bag and head to the living room where Jace is watching videos of AJ on YouTube.

"What are you watching?"

"Your boyfriend."

"Ha, very funny. Help me get ready, please! I'm starting to freak out because I feel like I'm gonna mess up my makeup." I think to myself. What kind of a makeup look am I going for? Dramatic winged eyeliner? No, that's too much for a first date. Ah, a date. A date with a K-Pop star. The nerves spread throughout my body and I feel sick to my stomach. Crap, I'm getting too into my head!

"Are you okay?" Jace asks. "You seem like you're on a different planet right now."

"Yeah, I'm okay but I'm getting all nervous again."

"You know what you need?" He sprints to the mini bar. "Some liquid courage."

I immediately think of the last debacle relating to alcohol and gag. "No. No. Take that devil's juice away from me. I'm still recovering from last time."

"Trust me, a shot won't do anything. It's like drinking water. It's also a quick cure for the nerves."

The more I thought about AJ, the more butterflies I got. "Screw it, give it to me." He hands me a mini vodka bottle, and I immediately grab it out of his hands and chug it.

"Whoa, you are nervous, aren't you? Normally your body rejects it."

"Today is a different story." I close my eyes, and try not to think about the aftertaste. I go back to the bathroom to brush my teeth and remove the repulsive taste. "Okay, I think I'm ready for my makeup." I grab my phone, and scroll through the explore page on Instagram for some inspiration. A moment later, I came across a picture of Kendall Jenner with a 90's model makeup look. That's it! It looks easy to do, but also sophisticated.

"What do you think about this makeup look? Would it go with my dress?" I flip my phone around to show Jace.

"That is perfect."

I grab my Anatasia makeup palette, an eyeshadow brush and dab onto a brown eyeshadow. I place it all over my lids, making windshield wiper motion in my crease. I move onto my eyeliner, and following that I apply some mascara on my eyelashes. Moving onto concealer, I apply some underneath my eyes, around my nose and start blending with my finger. Ah, my favorite -bronzer! With a light hand, I apply it all over my face to give myself that sunkissed glow. I finish it off with a brown lip liner and dab a brown-pinkish lipstick on my lips. I take a moment to scan myself in the mirror, and feel as if there's something missing. I mess around with my hair, and end up doing a middle part, allowing some of my front hair strands to frame my face. Then, I just clip the rest of my hair back with a claw clip - total 90s model vibe. I'm still not content though. What's missing? Ah, accessories! I run on my tiptoes to the room and open my accessories bag. I find these tiny gold dangling earrings that have a hint of black embellishment - very 'desi-like'. I mentally thank my Mom for bringing these from Pakistan. I put the earrings on, and head back to the living room where my heels are. Jace peeps from his phone screen, and does a double take as his mouth drops. He thrusts off of the sofa, and walks towards me.

"Who is this grown ass woman that I have never seen before?!" He twirls me around. "Wow, you look absolutely stunning. I'm quite speechless." He strokes my face and says, "If AJ wasn't taking you out on a date, I definitely would have." I blush and push his hands away.

"Yeah, okay. Sure." I roll my eyes. "How do I look?"

He pauses and stares at me like a proud parent. "Like a Pakistani princess." He smiles from ear to ear. "Shit, look at the time! It's almost eight. We gotta leave."

"We?" I tilt my head to the side.

"Yeah, I'm gonna be sitting at a table far from you, watching you guys."

"That's not creepy at all."

"It's not creepy, it's what best friends do. And also...this will be my entertainment for the night."

"I'm glad you find making myself look like a fool entertaining." We get ready to leave. I grab my purse, wear my heels and spritz a little perfume.

We make our way down to the lobby and towards the hotel bar.

"Okay, I'm gonna go in first, and then you follow so it doesn't look weird if he is already there." I tell him.

"That sounds good."

I head inside and straight to the bar. I sit on one of the barstools and instantly am greeted by the bartender.

"What would you like to drink?" He asks.

I'm still not really familiar with drinks so I place the safest bet. "Just any red wine, please. Can you put the tab on my hotel room?" He nods after I tell him the room number.

I turn back to see where Jace is sitting and he is literally three tables behind me, facing the entrance. He sees me and winks. As I'm jokingly scowling at him, his smile goes away and buries his face behind his phone.

"Here's your drink, Ma'm." The bartender sets down a napkin, with the glass on top of it.

"Thank you so much." Right when I take a sip of my wine, I hear the voice I've been waiting all night for.

"Hey, you." I turn around, and there he is. My God, he has a smile that stops hearts.

"Hi, you made it!" I get off of my stool, and lean in for a side hug. He reciprocates, thankfully. He smells so scrumptious, like a cologne model if that's a thing. He sits on the stool so effortlessly next to me. "Thanks for coming, what would you like to drink?" I ask.

"Oh, I actually don't drink." He replies. I felt a bit awkward, considering I was taking a sip of my wine as he said that.

"Yet you agreed to meet up for drinks." I act coy.

"Well, I wanted to see you again." I get butterflies as those words reach my ears.

"Well, you must order something. Juice? Soda?" I lay out options. The bartender approaches him.

"What will you have, Sir?" He asks. The bartender's eyes widen a little seeing AJ but he maintains his professional composure.

"Just some Sprite, thank you so much." AJ replies back politely.

When the bartender leaves to get his drink, his eyes land on mine and we giggle. Jesus, I feel like I'm back in high school by the way we are behaving.

"Why don't you drink?" I ask trying to divert from acting like teens.

"For work, I'm not really allowed to drink."

Wow, that's commitment. "Oh, I see. When was the last time you drank?"

"Like, probably three years ago, when I was twenty-two. I only took a sip of a drink, so I'm not sure if that counts as drinking. Does it?"

"No, it doesn't. Okay, well, when was the last time you 'drank, drank'?" As I ask that, the bartender places his drink in front of him and AJ thanks him.

"Ah, wow. I don't think I've ever gotten to that point. I've definitely gotten buzzed very few times, but never drunk. Although, I would love to know one day what it feels like. I always see people do funny things, and then later just blame it on the alcohol."

"Okay, calm down, Jamie Foxx." I joke, hoping that he'll catch the reference. He laughs uncontrollably, so I'm guessing he caught it.

"That was funny." He continues to laugh and proceeds to take a sip of his drink.

"I'm glad you caught that, or else I would have died of embarrassment." I start to feel the alcohol settling in. I should have eaten before I took that shot. No wonder it hit me this quickly, but Jace was right...it calmed my nerves.

"When was the last time you got drunk?" He asks.

"Funny you should ask." I laugh. " Like, two nights ago. My best friend got me super drunk since we had just finished our first semester of graduate school...which led to drunkenly buying tickets to Seoul and now we are here."

His eyes widen in disbelief. "No way! That's insane. What a night it must have been for you, and next morning."

"Well, I don't remember much from the night...but the morning, it was spent by me freaking out and yelling at him." I pause and look at him. I'm sitting in front of him right now because of that drunken night. I raise my glass, "Here's to drunken mistakes."

"Cheers to that." Our glasses clink as we toast. Shortly after, he looks over both of his shoulders. Is he worried?

"Is everything okay?" I ask.

"Oh, yeah. It's just...do you wanna get outta here?"

"What do you mean?" I think maybe he has the wrong idea of what I want the night to be like.

"Oh, it's just..." he pauses, "I thought I could show you a little bit of Korea. Are you hungry by any chance?" In the middle of his sentence, I feel my stomach rumbling.

"As a matter of fact, I am."

"Alright, perfect. I need to take you to this place which serves the best hot pot. Would that be something you'd like?"

"Oh, definitely." I take the last sip of my wine and start feeling a little more buzzed. "Is it okay if I quickly change?"

He examines me from head to toe and then back into my eyes. "You look great as it is, but yeah, go for it." He smiles.

I hop off of my seat as gracefully as I can, thank the bartender and look over at Jace. I widen my eyes hoping that he can telepathically talk to me. We lock eyes and I gesture to meet me in the hotel room. He nods back, gets up without hesitation and heads to the elevator. I lead AJ to the lobby.

"I'll be back real quick, so just wait here for a few minutes." I lightly touch his arm and instantly get butterflies. He returns the gesture by simpering at me.

"I'll be here." He sits on one of the lobby couches and I head upstairs.

Before I even take a small step into the room, Jace pounces at me. "HOW DID IT GO?!" The excitement in his voice is comparable to a child going to Disneyworld.

"It's still not over yet. I gotta quickly change. We are heading out to eat somewhere." I push him aside, and run to my suitcase. I take out some jeans, thermal leggings to wear under, a navy blue loose turtleneck, thigh high boots, and lastly grab my jacket.

"Okay, okay, loving this outfit actually. Very chic." Jace gives me the thumbs up.

"Thank you. Okay, I gotta go but don't wait up." I wink at him.

"Have fun!" He reciprocates.

I head down to the lobby as fast as I can. Wow, that only took me about five minutes and I look decent. The elevator doors open and he's not where I saw him last. I start looking around the area and still no sight of him. Did he leave?

"There you are." I hear his voice behind me.

"Oh, gosh. For a second there, I thought you left." I let out a sigh of relief.

"No, I wouldn't do that. I was standing by the elevator, but you didn't see me so I thought I'd have a little fun." He's in a very playful mood.

"Oh, I wouldn't care if you left." I roll my eyes, knowing I would definitely care.

"You wouldn't, huh?" He studies my lips and then meets his eyes with mine. Damn, butterflies, AGAIN! This is probably how all of his fans must feel.

"Yeah, I wouldn't. But, I'm glad you didn't leave because I really wanna try some hot pot." I laugh.

"I wouldn't leave." He pauses and grins. "Anyways, I ordered an Uber. Ready to go?"

"Yes, Sir." We head outside to see that the Uber is already there. AJ asks the driver if it's for him, and we get in the backseat. It's a little awkward because none of us are speaking. Instead, he's glancing at me through the corner of his eyes, and so am I. I keep telling myself to say something. Should I ask about his favorite movie? Song? Forget it. I'll wait for him to talk. As all these thoughts are going through my head, it turns out we are already at the place.

"Oh, it seems like we are here." He peeks out the window. He thanks the driver and we get out of the car. It's a very small restaurant at the corner of a dark street. Is he planning on murdering me? Is he like Dexter or something? Superstar during the day, serial killer at night.

We walk inside and there's no one here. The lights are dimmed, there are a couple of tables but all empty. A lady comes out from the room in the back and hugs AJ. Then she looks over at me and says hello. We follow her to a table towards the back corner and we sit. She hands over some menus and leaves. I'm so confused about this whole situation.

"There's no one here." My eyes peer through the place.

"Oh, that's because I reserved the whole place."

Excuse me?! He could just do that? "You did? Why?"

"I don't like having too many people around." His eyes are scanning through the menu. "Plus, I know the owners really well, so when they are closing but I want to come, they keep it open just for me. I really love this place, especially the owners. They always make me feel at home."

"That's really sweet of them, actually."

"Yeah, it is. Have you taken a look at the menu?" I take a look and realize I cannot read any of this. There are a couple of pictures but I have no idea what those even are.

"Yeah...the only problem is that I can't read any of this." We both laugh in unison.

"Okay, how about I just order and we can figure out what you like."

"I'm on board with that!" He looks over at the lady, and she comes over. He starts talking to her in Korean and she's jotting down everything he is saying then walks away.

"So, tell me about yourself." He crosses his arms on the table.

"What do you wanna know?" I ask and do the same.

"Okay, give me the basic details. Hometown, age, what you are studying...stuff like that."

"Well, how about I start off with my name. You still don't know it."

It takes a second for him to realize.

"Oh, crap. You're right. How come that hasn't come up yet?!"

"Maybe because you never asked." I laugh. "It's Zara. Zara Shah."

"Zara." He says my name and it sounds way more beautiful coming from his lips for some reason. "That's a beautiful name. It's like that clothing store, huh?"

"Yes, like the clothing store. You know, there were a million names out there to choose from, but my parents decided to name me the most basic name ever."

"Definitely not basic, I'll tell you that. I don't know any Zaras'. I'm happy that you're the first."

We both pause to admire each other. His eyes zero in on mine as if he's never seen a girl before. I won't lie, it's a warm feeling being the center of attention in someone's eyes...for once.

"Okay, your turn. What's your name?" His smile fades away a little. Shit, why did I ask him that?! He probably isn't ready to tell me who he is.

"AJ." Okay, maybe he is ready to tell me.

"Ah, that's better than my name."

"I completely disagree. Your name is so unique." As we argue about whether my name is deemed as somewhat special, our food arrives. There are different types of meat on a platter as well as vegetables.

"Wow, all of this looks amazing." I blankly stare at the food, realizing I have no idea how to cook any of this. "I'm not gonna lie...I've never done this before."

"Don't worry, I can teach you. I've been told I'm a great teacher." He winks

"I'll have you know, I'm a quick learner." I can be feisty too.

"Alright, if that's so...you have to cook the other half of the food."

"Deal." We shake hands in agreement. He starts putting some of the food into the pot.

"You still haven't told me about yourself." AJ says.

Yeah, I haven't because you keep distracting me with your charm!

"Alright, let's see. My name is Zara, I was born and raised in Los Angeles. I'm a twenty-five year old graduate student at USC, studying medicine. How's that?"

"Wow, you ARE a smart girl. I feel a bit inadequate." He feels inadequate?! Um, is he insane. I'm not the one who is known worldwide!

"Please, I'm not all that great."

"I don't know...I sense that there is more to you." He looks at me as if he's trying to find my soul through my eyes. "Why are you so fascinated with space?"

So, we are going deep here. I stop to think whether or not I should be open to him. I mean, I feel like I won't really see him after this trip, so what's the harm in being a little open?

"Ah, well. It goes back to when I was a kid. It's just such a long story."

"I'm listening." He looks at me attentively.

"Well, when I was a kid, there was a lot of stuff that happened. My parents had sponsored their siblings and their families to come to America. When there are so many families living together, a lot of drama is bound to happen. Most of my childhood consisted of my family members making things hard for my parents. There would be a lot of fights, yelling, and it was...very traumatic to say the least. I would get really scared, so I learned to console myself. I remember one time, my uncle started this argument with my Dad for no reason, and I always got scared of his voice. I just left the house and went into my backyard. I sat on my swing set and looked up. There were so many stars. I couldn't help but wonder what else might be out there, like other worlds. Eventually, my backyard became a place I would go to often. It became my safe haven. I would fantasize about leaving to another world. I'd look up at the stars as a way to escape whatever was happening at home. The screaming and yelling would blur out, and it would just be me, space and my imagination."

"It seems like you've been through a lot. I'm really sorry no one was there to comfort you." He reaches out and places his hand on top of mine while looking at me with empathic eyes. Just feeling his hand on top of mine gave me this strange sort of comfort that I haven't felt before.

"No, no. It's okay. I feel like that helped me grow a lot, although it also taught me to not rely on other people for comfort. My parents are great people, don't get me wrong. They were doing a great thing by helping people. I just don't think they realized how lonely, neglected and scared I've felt. I felt this way up until I met my best friend Jace. I think he was the first person in my life I really opened up to and allowed myself to lean on." For a moment, that feeling of sadness surfaces in my heart. I think he senses it too, which makes him grab my hand and give it a squeeze. "Anyways, enough of this sad talk. To answer your question, that's how my fascination about space grew. It makes me feel less lonely." I try to end the topic.

"I know what it's like to feel lonely. It's a very unsettling feeling, one that I have felt for years, so I understand where you're coming from."

Him, lonely? "What do you mean?" I ask. I genuinely want to know how a famous K-Pop star - who has adoring fans all over the world - feels lonely.

"Ah, it's a long story. Just know that I know the feeling." He seems hesitant to talk about it, so I just leave it at that. We start talking about random things, questioning each other about things we like or dislike. I attempt to cook the rest of the food like we agreed, but I fail so hard so he takes over which probably is best for both of our sakes. After about two hours, we finish dinner.

"Did you like it?" He asks.

"So, so much. This definitely won't be the last time I'll have hot pot." I am incredibly full. He kept putting so much food on my plate as if I was a child but I'm not complaining. Has he always been this nurturing?

"Wanna head back to your hotel?" He gets up and grabs his jacket.

"Yeah sure. Do we pay in the front?"

"Oh, it's already done."

When did he do that?!

"What? No, I wanted to get this as a thank you. I didn't even get the chance to fight over the bill!" A trait I inherited from my parents. They never let someone else pay without the 'fighting over the bill' dance.

"Well, even if you got the chance to, I would have won."

"How so?" I ask as I get out of my seat and put my jacket on.

He walks up to me, comes very close and says, "I would have just looked at you, very deeply into your eyes and...snatched the bill out of your hands." I think I stopped breathing for a second there and went into a trance. I snap out of it, leaving me a little flushed.

"I'm not easily distracted." I lie.

"You sure? Didn't seem that way just now." He smiles confidently. "I ordered the Uber, so it should be here soon." We thank the lady, and he gives her a hug before we step outside to see the Uber driver is already here.

He took care of everything, without me even knowing. He's so kind, generous, empathetic, funny, playful...qualities guys back in LA don't possess. Well, the guys that I know of. I'm so in awe of the person that he is. He seems WAY too good to be true.

Our car ride back so far is similar to how it was on the way to the restaurant. Except this time, I just couldn't stop thinking about when he put his hand on top of mine. It felt as if electricity went throughout my body. I wanted to feel that again so badly. I glance over at him. He's looking outside the window. His hand was resting on top of the seat, in very close proximity to mine. I keep thinking I should hold his hand. Is that too forward? What if he feels uncomfortable? Gosh, I wish I didn't overthink so much. "Just do it!" The voice in my head keeps reappearing. Screw it. I scoot my hand over and place my it on top of his. I can see from the corner of my eye that he looks at my hand, then at me. I'm looking straight ahead so I don't make eye contact with him. He takes his hand out from under mine. Shit, did he not like it? I look over at him and then he takes my hand and interlocks his with mine. His hand is rough, veiny and soft at the same time. I can feel my blood rushing to my face. He looks ahead and has the biggest smile on his face...same as me.

We reach the hotel after a couple minutes, which honestly seems like an hour. It felt as if time had stopped when he held my hand. We both get out of the car, but the Uber driver doesn't leave. I think he's taking this Uber back to his home.

"This is you." He has his hands in the pockets of his jacket. He keeps looking down and then back at me, as if he's nervous but he's trying hard to hide it.

"Thank you so much for an amazing night." I look down at my hands. "It's one that I'll never forget."

"This is definitely a date I'll always remember." He comes closer to me, slowly. He hasn't moved his eyes away from me. He comes so close, I can feel his breath on my lips. I can see him scan my lips, and then look in my eyes. Is he going to kiss me?! My heart starts to flutter, my stomach seems to have fireworks, and I forget to breathe. He closes his eyes, and leans in. My heart begins to pound the same way it did when I found the flight confirmation email, but this time in a way that feels really good. I close my eyes and feel him get closer and closer...and on cue, my phone rings! We both open our eyes and take a step back.

"Oh, uh. Sorry." I look at him embarrassed. Of course, my phone had to ring right when something was about to happen. I open my purse and start looking through to find my phone. I really need to clean it out - it looks like I stole Mary Poppins' purse and claimed it as my own. I start looking through more vigorously, and find my phone. Shit! My dad is calling me! I panic and right then, my bag falls down. Everything comes out. My phone, wallet, random receipts, chapstick, condoms...CONDOMS?! How the hell did these get here?! Now I know what Jace was putting inside of my bag! AJ looks at them with shock. His jaw drops and eyes widen. Oh, my god! The horror that is going through my veins at this moment is indescribable. I'm mortified. I have my Dad calling me, and the guy that I'm starting to like seeing all these condoms that make me seem like I had other plans in mind for tonight! He starts picking up the things that fell out of my bag, avoiding my eyes.

"It's not what you think." I look at him in panic.

"Uh, no it's okay." He replies back in that tone people have when trying to hide their judgment.

"I know for a fact my best friend put these in here as a joke. He does stupid stuff like that." I'm going to kill him.

Shortly after, my phone stops ringing, thank God.

"Anyways, don't worry about it. I've been meaning to tell you something all night. You see, I'm a K..." and as he was about to tell me that he's a K-Pop star, my phone rings again. It's my Dad, again, calling at the wrong time. Again. "You should get that, I'll wait."

"I'm so sorry." I feel so bad. "Hello?" I answer.

"Hello, Zara. How are you?"

"Hi, Dad. Uh, I'm good. I'm with my friends, is it okay if I call you later?"

"Oh, okay. That's fine. Your Mom and I were just going to ask if we should drop food at your apartment. We thought we'd call first before coming."

SHIT! I'm dead. "No, no! Dad, don't come. Thank you, but we made a lot of food here." Yeah, I totally don't sound suspicious.

"Uh, okay. Just let us know if you need anything."

"Okay, I will. Thank you, Dad. Give Mom my love! Bye!." That was probably the quickest goodbye I have ever said to anyone. I hang up and turn to AJ. "I'm so incredibly sorry about that. My Dad doesn't know I'm here."

"You're such a rebel." He winks.

"Yeah, you could say that. Sorry, you were saying something before hell broke loose." I chuckle.

"Oh, yeah, right. That. Well, okay." He pauses and musters up the courage to tell me. "I'm a K-Pop star in the band called NOWus." He lets out a sigh. "That's the reason I was being weird all night. I was afraid I would get noticed. I'm not exactly supposed to be out right now...but I really wanted to see you."

I didn't picture that I'd be at loss for words. What do I say? That I knew about it? Here I go again, overthinking.

"Oh my God. Wow, that's crazy." I try to act surprised. My palms get sweaty, my eyes wander off. Gosh, I'm a pretty bad liar. I think he can tell too by his quizzical expression.

"You okay?" He asks.

No, I'm not. But, I can't tell him that. "Yeah, I am." I reply nervously. I'm just gonna come clean. I can't keep this from him. "Actually...I knew that. Not when I met you, but after you left, my best friend told me who you were. I just didn't want to make you feel uncomfortable." I finally feel at ease telling him the truth. "In fact, I was even contemplating not seeing you tonight after I found out."

He's taken aback. "Why?"

I take a deep breath and sigh. "I just didn't think that someone as desired as you are, would like someone like me." Hearing that seems to upset him from the look on his face.

He comes closer, puts his hands on either side of my face, looks into my eyes and says, "I think I liked you the moment I saw you." Am I hearing this right? Almost immediately I felt overwhelmingly shy.

I take a step back. "Ah, you are good with your words." He lets go of me and takes a step back as well, but has this smug look on his face. He knows exactly what he's doing. He has this way of being both sensitive and sexy at the same time. "I'm going to go now, get some sleep. I'm surprised I'm not jetlagged." I slowly walk backwards, hoping he'd stop me. "Goodnight."

"Wait." He calls out. I stop walking and he runs to me. "I wanna see you again."

"That can be arranged. Here, take my number." He gives me his phone, and I save my number, with a blue heart next to my name.

"I have the next two days off. I want to spend it with you. I'll call you sometime tomorrow morning and we can plan something out."

"I can't wait." I reply back with an unhidden smile. I give back his phone and as he puts it back in his pocket, I lean in and kiss him on the cheek. I linger for just a moment. I pull back, and see a surprised expression on his face. I smile, turn around and start walking towards the hotel. Now THAT will keep him missing me.

I get to the hotel room, and see Jace watching T.V. and drinking in the living room. He gets up as soon as he sees me.

"Hey there, you little minx. How was your date?!"

"It was amazing." I take my jacket off, and sit next to him on the couch. " Jace, I don't think I've ever felt this way before."

"Like what?"

"Like, I think I'm falling in love."

CHAPTER SIX

You're a Star

After a long night of talking about AJ with Jace, I wake up in the morning feeling as if last night was just a dream. Getting out of bed quickly, rush to start my day. I never just how right love songs were until now. Excitement filled me, and I couldn't remember the last time I felt this way. "Time to wake up!" I jump on Jace. "Korea awaits!"

He cracks one eye open. "More like your boyfriend awaits. Let me sleep for another hour."

"Nope, we are on vacation, Jace! We can sleep once we are dead, but last time I checked, we are still above the ground." I pull the sheets off of him.

"Okay, calm down, Zara. If I knew a man made you this happy, I would have kidnapped a bunch back in LA and started your own bachelorette show."

"AJ is just not any man...he's different."

"Pretty sure he is still the same like the rest of us."

"Yeah, anatomically. His heart though...that's different. Well, so far."

"Damn, girl! I don't think I've ever seen you this smitten over a man before. I'm just waiting for you to start singing and birds joining you." He laughs.

I throw a pillow at him. "Okay, enough of your talk. Get in the shower and start getting ready. AJ is gonna call."

"When?"

"Well, I'm not sure. He said he'll call me sometime today to hang out." I start to worry that maybe he won't. Shrugging, I try and play it off. "Well, honestly, I don't even care if he calls. We will have fun regardless." I do care, but I don't want to show it.

"You do care. Stop lying."

"No I don't. I haven't even thought about him that much since I woke up." Another lie, again. At least every three seconds he pops in my mind. Just as I say that, I hear my phone ring. It's an unknown number.

"Oh my God, I think that's him!" I start jumping on the bed.

"Yeah, you totally don't care." Jace rolls his eyes and heads towards the shower.

I clear my throat, and answer. "Hello?" I try to downplay my enthusiasm.

"Hey, it's AJ." Just hearing him has me weak in the knees.

"Hey, you."

"Are you busy today?" He asks. Am I busy? For you, I have my whole day open.

"Not really, my friend and I were just going to do some sightseeing. Why? Anything in mind?"

"Well...yeah. I wanted to see you but something came up. So, my sister surprised me this morning. She wanted to come to my show, and so she hopped on a plane from Australia." He stops talking for a brief moment. "Would it be weird if she comes along with us? I swear, this isn't like some sort of 'meet the family' scheme." I can tell from the way he's speaking that he feels really bad.

"No, no. I wasn't going there but yes, I would love to hang out with her. Is it okay if my friend comes along?" Might as well play cupid.

"Yes, of course!" His voice lights up. "How about I pick you guys up in about an hour?"

"That sounds good to me."

"Perfect." He pauses. "Zara..."

62

"Yes?"

"I can't wait to see you." My heart flutters.

"Feeling is mutual. See you in an hour." I hang up and lie down. Gosh, I feel like I'm on cloud nine.

Jace comes out of the shower and sees me lying on the bed. "Bitch, are you okay?"

"I'm more than okay. I'm...I'm high."

"High off of what? We don't have any drugs."

"I meant, high off of LOVE!"

"You are so whipped." He grabs me off of the bed. "I'm putting your lovey-dovey ass in the shower."

"I can get in there by myself, thank you very much." I laugh and pull out of his grasp. "Oh, also...you're coming with us. He just called to make plans, and turns out his sister flew from Australia to surprise him, so she'll be coming along."

Jace considers. "Is she hot?" He asks.

"Yeah, totally." I hope he can hear the sarcasm in my voice. "Come on! I haven't seen her! You should know more than me."

"Oh, crap. You know what, I don't think I've ever seen a picture of her." He picks his phone off the nightstand and starts searching.

"No, stop, Jace! Don't look her up, it will kill the mystery. Just wait, who knows, what if you marry her?"

"I highly doubt that, but I don't mind showing her a good time in Korea...if you know what I mean."

"You're the worst, but I love you." I give him a kiss on the cheek and head to the bathroom to start getting ready. I shower, add a touch of makeup, and head to the living room, only to find a pile of his clothing on the floor and not him.

"Jace?" I look around.

"In the room!" I walk in and see him dressed up as if he was about to be in a fashion show, making me look like I got dressed by a teenager.

"Wow, you went all out." He's wearing a maroon button down, with black jeans, a black coat and black Timberland boots.

"I figured, go big or go home. Also...I'm a little nervous about meeting him for some reason."

I laugh. "Oh my God, don't be. He's really down to earth, in like a Godly manner."

"Zara, you don't understand." He can't stand still without fidgeting. "I'm his biggest fan! Not all of us have been living under a rock!"

"I promise you, you will be fine."

He sighs. "You're right. Just, maybe hold my hand when we see him?"

"Uh, I'm pretty sure he's gonna think something else if he were to see that."

"Shit, you're right. Damn, look at you being all loyal to him after one date."

"It was a hell of a date." I wink. Right then, I hear my phone ringing. I sprint over to the living room, and it's him!

"Hello?" I answer.

"Hey, there. It's me. I'm outside!"

"Oh, okay! We will be in the lobby in about five minutes " I hang up. Jace comes outside, looking like a deer in head-lights. "Okay, Jace. You have about five minutes to get yourself together! He's here!" It seems like we both are frea-king out. Him with panic, me out of excitement.

"Alright, alright. I'm good, I'm ready. Let's roll." He fixes his posture, takes a couple deep breaths, cracks his neck and heads to the door. "You coming?"

"I might." We both laugh and head down.

I start getting butterflies the closer we get to the lobby door. I see him standing outside the car, just looking perfect as usual.

"Oh. My. God." Jace stops in his tracks.

"I know, isn't he so dreamy?"

"Bitch, not him. Her!" I look back at AJ and see this gorgeous, Victoria Secret model-like human being standing next to him. AJ sees me through the glass doors. By the time I step outside, he's standing right in front of me.

"Hey there, beautiful." Awe, he thinks I'm beautiful.

"Hey, how you doin'?" I channel my inner Joey from Friends. Everyone stops and stares at me, but AJ laughs.

"You've just become my favorite person." AJ pulls me in for a quick tight hug. "Zara, this is my sister Areum."

"You can call me Ari, just to save you the trouble." She prances towards me and gives a welcoming hug. "My brother has been talking about you all morning."

"Oh, has he now?" I see him blush.

"Ahem." Jace coughs.

"Oh, everyone, this is my best friend Jace, also the reason why we are here."

"I've heard a lot about you." AJ reaches out for a handshake. I know Jace is dying inside but surprisingly is keeping it cool.

"All good things, I hope." We all laugh as Jace looks over at me while shaking AJ's hand. Jace turns to Ari, and his expression is priceless. He activates his charming side.

"May I just say...you are absolutely breathtaking, Ari." He acts like a knight in shining armor by bowing and kissing her hand.

"As long as it's coming from your lips, you can say whatever you like." She grins. Both mine and AJ's jaws drop.

"Anyways..." AJ tries to break up the sexual tension between the two. "I was thinking we can go to a few places. First, to Bukchon Hanok Village. It's super close by and I think you'd really like it, Zara. Is everyone okay with that?" Both Ari and Jace nod in agreement, but I think they could care less right now. We walk to the car, and AJ steps into the driver seat.

"You sit in the front seat, Zara. I'll sit in the back with Jace." These two need to get a room. I don't mind it at all, because I get the best view of AJ. I cannot get enough of this man. AJ starts driving, and holds my hand so nonchalantly. I wonder if there is anything that he can do that won't give me butterflies.

We get to Bukchon Hanok Village, and AJ parks on the side of the street. The roads are so narrow, I don't know how there can be a two way traffic. We step out of the car, and the cold breeze gives me goosebumps all over my body.

"Welcome to Bukchon Hanok Village." AJ gestures, showcasing the street we parked on as if it's an artifact at a museum. He seems more excited about it than any one of us. We start walking. There's almost no one else around.

I pull out my phone to take pictures of the architecture in amazement. There are many alleys, with small shops around. AJ explains that the village is six hundred years old. People did a phenomenal job preserving it. It feels as though I have traveled back in time. The neighborhood has traditional houses that people actually still live in! If I lived here, I'd feel as if I'm in a Disney movie.

"Let's take pictures!" AJ takes out his phone. He places his hand around my waist, pulls me closer and snaps a few photos. In the midst of our little photoshoot, we realize Jace and Ari aren't near us. "Where did these two go?" AJ and I start looking around and find them making out in the corner of an alley!

"Should we scare them?" I suggest with an evil smile on my face.

"I was just about to ask you that!" AJ and I hide on the side of the building that they are making out against. We swiftly jump out and scream, startling them. AJ runs over to Jace and gives him a playful hug. Ari is red as a tomato, but is trying to keep her composure by laughing along. "Seems like you two are enjoying the buildings!"

"Well, we were!" Jace laughs. He glances at Ari and holds her hand. It's actually so heartwarming seeing Jace like this. I've seen him be flirty with people, but not in this way. It seems more than just lust.

The four of us take more pictures up until Jace asks about eating. Honestly, I completely forgot about not having eaten yet from all the fun I'm having. AJ takes us to Gwangjang Market and as soon as we step outside the car, we are welcomed by the intense aroma of the food. The place is bustling with people everywhere. AJ puts on a face mask. I'm a little puzzled at first, but I think he doesn't want to be recognized.

He makes me try all his favorite foods like bindaetteok, bibimbap, and gimbap. The flavors are sensational. My taste buds were having the time of their lives. It felt like I was on one of those food channels, traveling around and sampling everything! AJ is hand feeding Jace and Ari at times as if they are children. It was the cutest sight to see.

I stop eating and take a moment to admire him. He is so incredibly loving, and affectionate. The whole time, he was trying to make all of us laugh, even if it meant that he made a fool out of himself. He didn't care as long as we all got a laugh out of it. He's dorky, bubbly, vivacious, and sensitive but has this sexy side to him that only I get to see.

"Earth to Zara!" Jace snaps his fingers in front of my face. "What were you thinking about?"

Thanks, for putting me on the spot, Jace.

"Uh, nothing. Just thinking about how delicious this food is."

"You sure you're talking about food?" They all try to keep their laughs at a minimum so I'm not as embarrassed.

"Yes, I AM talking about food." I try to save myself. Jace and Ari start talking amongst themselves and AJ turns to me.

"It's getting a little dark now, which is the perfect time to take you to Dongdaemun. We can go for an evening stroll."

"What about these two?" I ask.

"I think these two deserve some alone time." He laughs. "So do we." He looks at me with a seductive smile. I swear, he has multiple personalities but I mean it with the best connotation.

We finish eating and head back to the car. Jace pulls me aside and we slow our pace for a moment.

"So, I wanna take her to the hotel and get to know her more."

"You mean...sleep with her?!" I may have said it a bit loud, but thankfully Ari and AJ didn't hear me since they are walking a bit further from us.

"Shh, you're so freaking loud, Zara!" He elbows me and whispers. "But, no. I actually just want to talk to her and get to know her. I think... I am falling in love."

"I think you're experiencing lust at first sight."

"No, bitch. It's love...maybe a little lust. I just wanna run my fingers through her..."

"Shut up, they're looking at us." Both AJ and Ari were waiting for us by the car. Damn, they walk fast. We all get inside and AJ starts driving to Dongdaemun.

"So, Jace and I are going to go to the hotel once we get there. Is that okay?" Ari asks. AJ has a stern expression on his face, which only lasts for a few seconds.

"Yeah, that's fine by me. You two have fun." He looks over to me and smiles. "Me and Zara have plans of our own." Plans of our own? Does that include us staring at each other and making out passionately, because I'm on board with that.

We get to Dongdaemun, AJ parks the car and I don't know how or when but Jace had already ordered an Uber, which is parked across the street from us. He and Ari rush over to the car and leave. AJ wears his mask again and we stride along a sidewalk. On our right, there is a manmade river, and to the left there's a wall covered in vines. It emits a very romantic vibe, no wonder he wanted to take me here. We sit down on one of the benches which overlooks the river.

"It's absolutely incredible." I admire the beauty surrounding us.

"It certainly is."

Glancing over, I see he's looking at me, smiling with his eyes. Quickly I look away, trying to hide my cheeks which I feel heating up.

We sit there in silence for a moment. I appreciate the calmness that is overtaking me. I'll remember this forever.

"Zara?" AJ breaks the silence.

"Yeah?"

He takes off his mask. "I'm...really happy right now."

"I'm really happy, too." I lightly smile. I think my eyes can speak for themselves as to how I'm feeling. "I'm really glad you decided to help me yesterday, or else we both wouldn't be here."

He laughs. "You wanna know the truth?"

"What truth?"

"You know yesterday, I said I liked you the moment I saw you. Remember that?"

"Uh-huh..."

"I wasn't lying. When you walked in, I had my eyes glued to you. I didn't realize what I was thinking at that moment, was actually coming out of my mouth. My friend - whose name is Lee by the way – he heard it though."

"What did you say?"

"I said 'wow' when I saw you. Lee was surprised because he knows no one catches my attention like that, so he dragged me to you. I was really nervous, I don't know if you caught that."

Him, a K-Pop prince, nervous to talk to me?!

"I didn't. I just figured you were really shy. Plus, I was too much in the middle of a freak out to notice anything at all."

"I thank the stars that I was there at the right time. If I came a few minutes later, I would have missed you. You know, I've been smiling since yesterday? Even my team members noticed. Like, I'm usually always smiling but I don't know...I guess if they can sense something is different about me, then it must be true."

I'm beaming as I'm hearing all this. I feel so...special.

"You're not alone." I caress his hand. We both gaze at each other. I get lost into his eyes. There's something about them. They speak more than his words. I don't know what it is, but it seems as if his eyes hide something...a sort of sadness. I remember what he said yesterday about how he knows what loneliness feels like, and I want to know more. "AJ, can I ask a personal question?"

"Sure."

"You don't have to answer if you don't feel comfortable, okay?"

"Just ask, it's okay. I trust you." My heart warms up hearing that.

"Yesterday, you said you know what it feels like to be lonely...what did you mean by that?" His smile fades.

"It's a long story." He looks down.

"I'm listening." I comfort him.

"Gosh, where do I begin." He exhales. "I came to Korea at a very young age to be a trainee. I was about fourteen years old. I didn't speak the language too well, and I didn't know anyone around here."

"You came here all alone?"

"Yeah. My parents got me settled in and everything, but since then I've kind of been on my own. It's just...this life isn't as glamorous as it seems. It's lonely, and extremely taxing, both emotionally and physically. There are strict rules I have to follow. Like, I have to watch what I eat and drink. Alcohol is out of the question. I can't even choose where I live. Oh, and I...can't really be out with a girl either. I was away from my family all these years. Whenever I had a problem, I didn't have my parents to turn to and ask for their advice. It's kind of like, I had to become my own parent and learn what's right from wrong. I suffered from depression and anxiety, and didn't tell a soul, not even my family because I didn't want them to worry. Like you, I also have had to learn to comfort myself."

I start to get teary eyed, and look down to hide it from him.

AJ continues, giving my hand a squeeze, "I missed out on so many life experiences that any normal person goes through...having birthday parties, first love, first heartbreak, those sort of things. There were times where I just wanted to give up, especially when I'd be close to debuting each year. I was a trainee for seven years, which is such a long time and it was not easy. There was a strict schedule. It felt a little like I was in the military, but with singing and dancing, and no room for mistakes. I'd watch all these trainees come in and get debuted in such a short amount of time...it made me think at times that maybe I don't have what it takes."

I can feel the pain in his voice as he's speaking. I wish I could go back in time and just take it all away.

"Look where you are now, AJ. You're so young and already so successful. You should be so proud of yourself."

"I know and I'm thankful for that. I just...sometimes wonder if all of those sacrifices were worth it."

"If I were in your shoes, I don't think I would have lasted. I mean, that sounds incredibly hard."

"I mean, this is the career path I chose...so I can't exactly complain. I just wanted it SO badly. I didn't care what I had to go through. I couldn't give up, even when it seemed tempting at times." He looks out in the distance. "Eventually, I got to live out my dream. I have my amazing team members, who honestly saved my life. I would die for them. Even now, after debuting, things haven't been the easiest. It's a lot of hard work, and I can't afford to be irresponsible. I wouldn't be the only one who faces the consequences, but also my whole group. As a leader, it's almost like I have to be perfect. I rarely show how much I'm struggling to my team members...I don't want them to see me as weak or worry about me in any way.

71

I'd rather take care of others than the other way around, you know?"

"We all need someone to take care of us, just a little." I hold his hand tighter.

"I can never ask that from anyone."

"You don't have to ask...people who love you would want to be there for you during hard or happy times." I see his eyes get glassy as if he's about to cry. I move closer, and hug him. He hugs me even tighter and holds onto me for a while. I thought I went through an ordeal when I was younger...but hearing his story broke my heart. The days he should have been worry-free, he was suffering from so much pain. I guess it is true what they say...people who smile the most, are the ones that are the saddest.

He looks away and seems to wipe his tears. "Anyways, enough about this. I'm happy, especially right now." He looks up at the sky and then at me. "You're a star." He brushes his thumb against the side of my cheek.

"Well, you're a superstar. Yes, pun intended."

We both laugh really loudly. I think he needed it after this whole conversation.

"I love the night sky. There's just something about the night time, don't you agree?" He puts his head back to get a better view of the night sky.

"Yeah. I've always been nocturnal for as long as I could remember. I don't know what it is...there's this comfort during the night that I don't feel during the day time. It's relaxing. I feel like we are most vulnerable at night and the most creative."

He sits back up. "Wow, I don't think I've met someone before who takes words right out of my mouth."

"I feel like...you and I are very similar. I mean, I still feel like I don't know everything about you, but from what I've gathered, it seems like you just understand everything that I say without having to explain too much. I hope you feel the same way."

"I do...I wouldn't have shared this much with you if I didn't feel that way." He stares at me like he's trying to capture every feature of my face. "I wanna show you something." He swiftly grabs my hand and starts walking fast.

"Where are we going?"

"You'll see." We start approaching a bridge. "Okay, close your eyes."

"Are you trying to throw me over the bridge?" I joke.

"Just, close your eyes." He places his hands over my eyes and whispers in my ears. "Do you trust me?"

"I do." I felt like Princess Jasmine from Aladdin for a moment. He starts guiding me slowly. I keep praying I don't trip and fall in front of him. We come to a halt after a few steps.

"Okay, open your eyes." He uncovers my eyes.

"Wow."

Speechless does not even begin to describe how I feel. The view from this bridge is just...stunning. I can see tall buildings and the lights within them are twinkling like stars. The river is just beneath us, centered as if it were in a painting. The sky is clear of clouds and the full moon illuminates everything it touches.

"Do you like it?" I can feel his body get closer to mine.

"I...love it."

I love everything about it, especially him. I feel his lips against the back of my head. He moves my hair to the side, kisses my neck. Closing my eyes, I feel goosebumps throughout my body. His lips are so soft and plump. Time slows to a stop.

"Do you want to start heading back?" He whispers in my ear.

"Maybe..." I whisper back, eyes still closed.

"Not sick of me yet?" I feel his hands slowly tightening around my waist.

"Not even the slightest." I could die here, right now and be satisfied. As I'm indulging every second of this moment, my phone rings. I snap back to reality. I hope it's not my Dad! I take my phone out of my purse, only to see it's Jace calling.

"Perfect timing." I growl.

"Bitch, where are you guys?" He asks.

"We are still at Dongdaemun."

"Oh, okay. I was calling because Ari needs to go to her hotel, and I figured when AJ drops you off here, he can just pick her up."

"Yeah, that sounds good. I'll tell him."

"Alright, I'll see you soon, you dirty little..." and before he finishes his sentence, I hang up.

"Ari wants to go back to her hotel, so we should probably head back." He frowns. I feel the same way inside.

"Ah, okay." He puts on his mask, and then holds my hand as we walk back to the car.

Before we reach the hotel, I call Jace to let them know we are close by and to come down. I'm already getting exceptionally sad that the night is ending. I can sense that he is too from the way he is holding my hand so firmly. When we get to the hotel, both of them are standing outside.

"Awe, man. I won't get to kiss you goodbye." AJ sounds disappointed.

"Kiss me, huh?"

"Yeah, in case you haven't realized... I've been wanting to do it for a while."

"I guess you'll just have to wait a little longer." Leaning over, I give him a kiss on the cheek before we get out of the car. His cheeks turn cherry red. I love that I can affect him in this way...let's just say, it's a slight ego boost.

"Hey, you two. Have fun?" Ari wraps her arm around my neck.

I look at AJ and back at her. "We sure did. Did you two have FUN?" I emphasize to Jace and Ari.

Both stare into each other's eyes and Jace replies, "We sure did."

Ari winks and kisses Jace goodbye, making her way to the car.

"Ari and I are going to this place tomorrow evening, which is kind of like a bar. We usually go there when she visits since she loves it. It's a very 'small town college' vibe. Would you two want to join?" AJ asks.

"It's a hell yes from me, man!" Jace high-fives him.

"And, you?" AJ turns to me, and displays slight puppy dog eyes.

"On one condition." I smirk. "You have to dance with me to at least one song."

"Deal." He lifts my face to meet his eyes. "I wish tomorrow was here already." He kisses my forehead, and heads to the car.

I hate seeing him walk away from me. If I already feel this deeply about him...what am I going to do when I have to leave in a few days?

CHAPTER SEVEN

Come My Way

"Zara, wake up! Are you okay?!" My eyes open abruptly from Jace shaking me.

"Yeah, why?"

"You were crying in your sleep."

"What do you mean?" I'm taken aback.

"I mean, you were literally crying in your sleep, minus the tears. You were so loud, it woke me up."

"Oh, man. I don't know why I would be crying." I try to think back to what I was possibly dreaming about. Then I remember just a little...it had to do with AJ.

"Maybe you dreamt that your parents found out you lied to them, and you were trying to ask for forgiveness." I can't tell if he's trying to make a joke or if he's serious.

"That definitely wasn't it." I get out of bed, grab a bottle of water and chug as if I hadn't drank water in days. "It was about AJ."

Jace raises his eyebrows. "Why would you be crying about him?" After a few seconds, realization leaves a frown on his face. "Are you sad about leaving?"

I nod. "Bingo." I can't hide the sheer sadness.

"Awe, Zara." Jace runs his fingers through my hair. "I know how you're feeling. I feel the same way about Ari."

"I don't wanna feel this!" I cover my face with my hands.

"Neither do I, but here we are." He forcefully pulls my hands off, and sits me down on the edge of the bed. "I know it will be heartbreaking when we leave, but just try to make the most out of it. Okay?" I reluctantly nod. "How did last night go? What did you two talk about?"

My heart sinks thinking about what he divulged last night. "He talked about his life. It was absolutely heartbreaking."

Jace becomes curious. "What about his life? His stardom?"

"Just how it all started. He talked about being on his own since he was fourteen, and how he struggled emotionally. We actually seem to have quite a bit in common."

"Like what?"

"Like...he missed out on a lot of life experiences, and so did I. Well, not more than him. He also learned to comfort himself because no one was around to do so. He was adamant about the fact that he can't be irresponsible because his actions could mean that his team will suffer the consequences. It's kind of like my culture, you know? I can't venture out and be a little disobedient because it will reflect on my family if just one rumor spreads. Gotta thank collectivist cultures for that!"

"Yeah, that's really rough. You know what I've been wondering though?" Jace draws his eyebrows together.

"What?"

"How has he been able to come out to see you? From what I remember, K-Pop stars aren't really allowed to date for a couple years after debuting. Apparently, fans get pretty upset if they find that one of their idols is dating. I don't even think they're even encouraged to interact with their friends. They just focus on work. He must really like you if he's secretly coming out to see you."

I recall the night of our first date. It all makes sense. "Ah, now I know what he meant when he said he wasn't supposed to be there…" I start to feel really guilty thinking that he's going behind people's backs just to see me. I mean, that's the definition of being irresponsible...but for him to take that risk, for me? How can I mean this much to him?

"Do you have a bedazzled coochie or something? He seems to be ready to risk it all!" Jace tries to lighten up my mood.

"You know, he hasn't even kissed me yet. Lady parts are out of the question."

"Maybe show him a little something tonight."

"Ew, no. Stop being gross." I get really flustered.

"I'm not being gross! Come on, you know you want to pounce on that..."

"Stop. Don't even finish that nasty sentence of yours."

Jace laughs uncontrollably from seeing how uncomfortable I was getting. "Okay, I'll stop but listen...we are going to leave in a few days. Like we said on the plane, we are living in the moment! You like this guy, and he likes you back. You know how rare this shit is?! If it gets to that point, just give it a chance. He doesn't seem the type that would break your heart."

"Won't break my heart? Wow, you're awfully confident."

"I have full faith in him. You should, too."

I take a minute to think. "I did say I would think less and do more..."

"Yes, bitch. DO HIM! That's what I've been trying to tell you. You are basically living every fan's wet dream right now."

A very conceited smile creeps up on my face. He is right...I am living every fan's fantasy.

***

Jace and I spent the day going to Gyeongbokgung Palace and Myeong-dong, where I picked up a very flowy dress to wear tonight. I realized I only packed the blue dress that I wore on my first date with AJ. We were exhausted after walking around so much. The only thing that is giving me the energy that I need is knowing I will see AJ soon. I find myself daydreaming about dancing with him. He can be my Patrick Swayze for the night.

Jace rummages in his suitcase and holds something up. "I figured you might actually need these tonight." He displays different colored condoms in his hands.

"Jesus, Jace!" I move his hands away from me. "By the way, don't think I didn't see those condoms that you graciously left in my purse! That shit was so embarrassing when it fell out right in front of AJ. He probably thought I was expecting a different type of meat that night other than the hot pot."

"I did that as a joke! Oh, I am so happy that happened. I swear, I think God is on my side."

"I wish God could stuff something in your mouth right now to shut you up."

"I mean...maybe tonight."

"Speaking of tonight, we should start getting ready. I think we have to meet up with them at the place. Did Ari text you the details? I haven't heard from AJ."

"Yeah, she did. She sent me the address and the name of the place. I say we leave in an hour."

Now I begin to wonder...why hasn't AJ texted me yet? I figured he would send me the details, not Ari. Maybe I'm overthinking again. I'm sure he's busy and just asked Ari to do it instead. That seems to be a logical explanation that my brain can't grasp. I brush off my thoughts, and begin getting ready. Jace beats me to the bathroom, so I start gathering my outfit, my shoes, makeup and curling iron.

***

"How do I look?" Jace shows off his outfit. He's dressed up in a white button down, with black slacks.

"You look like a Justin Timberlake knockoff." I cackle.

"Very funny. Really, how do I look? Should I change?"

"No! You look hot. How about me?" I twirl around.

"You look very beautiful. I'm loving this dress. It shows off those curves you've been hiding. Oh, wear your thigh high boots with it!"

I struggle a little putting on the boots, but he's right. It makes the whole outfit come to life. I make some final touches on my makeup, and wear my black 'churiyan', which are bangles in Urdu.

"Our Uber is here!" I hear Jace hollering from the door.

I take one final look and shriek out of excitement.

"Man. It's taking us about forty minutes to get there?!" Jace sounds disappointed as he looks at his phone.

"I gotta wait forty minutes to see him?!"

"You've waited twenty-five years to see him, I think forty minutes shouldn't be a problem."

After what seems like an eternity, we finally get to the bar. My palms start sweating. Damn it, why are my merocrine glands out of control right now?! I try to calm myself down by taking deep breaths. I shouldn't be this nervous anymore, but I am. Is this normal?

"Zara, you gotta get out of the car."

Jace seems slightly irritated, probably because I have been sitting here for about a minute.

"Okay, okay. I'm getting out. Sorry, I didn't realize I was frozen. I'm just so nervous, I don't even know why."

"You're in love, that's why." He looks straight ahead as we walk to the bar. He opens the door, and I see AJ and Ari sitting in the back corner. AJ was right, this does have a college town vibe. The lights are very dim, there's a dance floor right when you enter, with the bar behind it, surrounded by wooden tables. AJ's eyes meet mine as we approach the table and he gets up.

"Hey, you." We exchange an awkward hug, which is completely opposite from his previous hugs. Jace and Ari immediately start giving quick small kisses and sit next to each other. AJ moves over to make room for me in the booth. He's so quiet. I start getting a little anxious because of his withdrawn behavior.

"Hey, are you okay?" I ask him.

"Uh, yeah." He replies back but I'm not buying it.

"I know I haven't known you for too long but I think I know you enough to sense that something is wrong."

He lets out a sigh. "Zara..."

He pauses and I already know I don't wanna hear the end of this sentence.

"I feel like I have been completely irresponsible. You probably don't know this but I'm not exactly supposed to be doing all this - going out, dating. I've been lying to my manager about where I have been. I told my group members about you...and they've been lying for me as well. I just feel bad, they shouldn't be the ones protecting me. That's my job." He sounds frustrated.

"I wish I had the right words to say right now, which would make you feel better but...I think your group members are looking out for you because they love you. Maybe you should let them. It will make them feel better knowing that it was worth it because at least you get to be happy. You are happy, right?"

"I am." He lets out a smile in defeat. "I really, really am." He comes closer and gives me a quick peck on my cheek.

"Then just indulge in it. I'm leaving in a few days...then after that, you can go back to being your responsible self." Am I really preaching this to him? I can be such a hypocrite.

"We need to get this party started! I'm ordering us a round of shots. AJ, you're drinking! I don't care about what your K-Pop peeps have told you, you're letting loose tonight!" You would think that's coming out of Jace's mouth, but it was Ari. These two are practically the same person.

"I don't know if I should." AJ is hesitant but also seems like he might be convinced. "I'll take one shot, only!"

"I'll take it!" Ari exclaims in joy. She frolics over to the bar, and brings back eight shots.

"Eight shots? I thought we were just doing one round for now!" The taste of vodka from the night at Traditions resurfaces in my mouth.

"Yeah, the first round, we only drink two each!" Ari starts passing around the shot glasses. I can see why Jace is so enamored by her. Both are the life of the party.

"You are a goddess." Jace kisses her.

"Here's to an unforgettable night with unforgettable people!" Ari raises her shot glass, and we all follow. AJ and I gag a little, while Jace and Ari are already ready to drink the second one.

"Come on, Zara! Take the second shot with us." Jace slides my shot glass towards me.

"I promise I'll take it in a bit, unless you're willing to clean up my puke."

"Nah, I ain't about that life right now." Jace raises his glass to make a toast. "This is for AJ's concert!" He and Ari guzzle it down.

"Oh, you two are coming?" AJ's face brightens.

"Yeah, actually I bought the tickets before we came here and before she knew who you were. Now, I'm sure she won't miss it."

"I hope she doesn't." AJ moves even closer to me, and places his hand around my waist. It's funny how quickly his attitude changed from the moment I arrived compared to now. Will he continue to be like this for the rest of my trip? I can't help but wonder.

"I promise she won't miss it, especially if you convince her through some aegyo."

"Aegyo?" I question.

AJ laughs embarrassingly and plants his face in his hand. "No, no. I'm not doing that."

"What is it?" I ask again. It sounds like a type of egg dish.

"Ah, it's this cute behavior-like thing K-Pop stars have to do. It's funny but it can be a little embarrassing!"

"Do it." I challenge him.

"If I do, would you still like me?"

"That depends. If it's really bad, I might still like you out of pity."

"Here goes nothing then!" He takes a deep breath, looks down, then back up and lets out a baby sound while making a puppy dog face. I burst out laughing.

"Okay, that was really cute in a slightly disturbing way!" I place my hand on the back of his head, and pull him closer against my cheek. He looks so humiliated, I feel so bad.

"So, do you still like me?" He asks.

"A lot more, promise." I lay a kiss on his cheek.

"The DJ is taking song requests!" Ari leaps out, and drags Jace along with her to the DJ booth. I see Jace look back at me and give a devilish smirk. Oh, no. What is he planning on doing? Both come back and I try to telepathically talk to him with my eyes. He isn't responsive, which starts to worry me. I just never know what Jace's wicked mind is up to. Nelly Furtado's song 'Promiscuous' ends, and the next song plays. My jaw slightly opens, my eyebrows rise up, and I look directly at Jace, who is smiling as if his evil plan was accomplished. 'Come My Way' by PLVTINUM is playing! Is he trying to make my dream come true, literally?! I shake my head and laugh.

"AJ, this is Zara's favorite song." Jace is a mastermind. I know exactly what he's doing.

83

"Oh, is it now?"

At that moment, I decided to live out my dream. Screw it! I grab the second shot, and down it. Everyone stares at me as they are unable to understand what just got into me.

"AJ, you owe me a dance." I grab his hand, without even asking for his permission. From his facial expression, I can tell he is stunned by this side of me. Honestly, so am I. We make our way to the dance floor, and I feel my inner goddess coming out as the alcohol settles in. I place my arms around his neck, and slowly glide my hands down his chest to his abs. I can feel how hard his abs are, and I start picturing how he would look shirtless. I take his hands and move them against the sides of my body, making him feel my curves.

We have this insatiable hunger in our eyes for one another. I gracefully turn around, and start grinding my body against him, pressing his hands against my hips. Both of us are swaying in sync to the music. When the slow part of the song comes up, he turns me around briskly so that my lips are aligned with his. He puts his hand at the nape of my neck and pulls me in closer. His eyes glance at my lips, then into my eyes. My heart starts palpitating. We both breathe heavily. He gets closer, and closer and I feel his lips slightly brush against mine. This is the moment I have been waiting for. The most desired kiss in history of my life. We close our eyes and...hear a scream! What now?! Does God not want me to kiss this man?!

We look around to see where the scream came from. It's by the bar area where people are gathering around. AJ stays back, but I rush over and see Jace is already by the man who collapsed on the floor.

"Jace, what happened?"

"He just fell down. I tried to shake him to see if he's conscious, and he's not."

"I'll check to see if he's breathing." I listen over his mouth and nose for breathing sounds.

"He has gasping breaths, Jace. I think he went into cardiac arrest. We need to perform CPR, ASAP!"

"I can't do it, I drank more with Ari. You have to!"

"Okay, tell Ari to call an ambulance." I don't even hesitate and start chest compressions. A few minutes pass, and the ambulance still hasn't arrived. In my head, I keep thinking this person might die but that motivates me to keep going. Each second feels like a minute. "Jace, tell Ari to call again." I start getting anxious. My forehead is sweating from the effort and stress. Please, God. Do not let this man die. I start reciting prayers. My arms are tired but I can't stop. The man starts gasping a little bit more. It's working! Thankfully, right then the paramedics arrive but I continue the chest compressions until they come over. Ari starts speaking to them in Korean, explaining what happened. They take over, one of the paramedics pats me on the back and takes him into the ambulance.

Sitting on my heels, I don't even know how to feel. I didn't feel the intensity of the situation at the moment, but it starts to hit me now. I tear up a little. I feel a hand on my shoulder, it's AJ. He pulls me in for a hug, and I hold onto him tightly.

"You're shaking." He kisses my forehead.

""The paramedic told me that you might have just saved that man's life." Ari tries to calm me down as well.

"You did well, Zara." Jace brushes the back of my hair.

I don't say much. I'm still in shock as to what just happened but also relieved to know I was able to be here to help this man. This is the reason why I chose medicine.

All four of us decide to leave after what just happened. We head outside the bar, and Jace pulls me aside.

"Is it okay if I spend the night at Ari's hotel?"

"Yeah, of course. Go for it."

He squints his eyes as if he's unsure if my response is genuine. "Are you sure you'll be okay?"

"Yeah! I'm not a child, idiot." I give a gentle tug on his arm.

"Why don't you have AJ take you back to the hotel?"

"Uh...I don't know. He probably has to go back home."

"Bitch, hold up." He moves me away and walks towards AJ.

"Hey, AJ. Do you mind taking Zara back to the hotel? Ari and I are going to hang out."

I patiently wait for AJ's response, hoping he'll agree. "Of course, I'll take her. I was planning to anyway." Hearing that made me feel so...loved and protected. Jace and AJ order an Uber for our respective destinations. Our Uber driver comes first. Jace stops me before I get into the car.

"Zara, don't think too much about what happened. Remember, you did really well. You saved someone's life. Just take the rest of the night to be with AJ. Okay?" Jace hugs and kisses the top of my head. "Also, if you need some love gloves, they are inside one of the drawers of the right nightstand." I don't even fight back and just laugh. I needed him to make one of his dirty jokes right about now.

***

"I need a shower." I throw my hotel key on the table.

"Are you okay?"

"Yeah, I am." I try to sound convincing.

"I know I haven't known you for too long but I think I know you enough to sense that something is wrong."

I smile because he's using the same line I used earlier.

"Using my own lines against me, huh?"

"Figured it would make you smile a bit. You didn't say a word on the car ride back, so I've been worried this whole time."

"I'm fine. I just need to shower this night off." I go to my room, grab my pjs and head to the bathroom.

When I come out, I find AJ sitting on the couch, with a bottle of champagne waiting on the table and music playing on the Apple T.V.

"What's all this?"

"Well, you just saved your first patient today. I thought we'd celebrate."

"This is really nice." He hands me a glass and I take a sip. "I still don't know if the man survived though."

"Funny you mention that...I just got off the phone with the hospital and he's stable. They said that he will make a full recovery, thanks to you."

I get this overwhelming sense of relief and tears trickle down my cheeks.

"No, no why are you crying? I thought it would make you happy." He takes the glass out of my hand and sets it on the table.

"No, it did. So much. It just happened so fast, I was just worried that I may have done something wrong which would've cost him his life."

He gently caresses my face, and wipes away my tears. "He's alive, Zara. Okay?" He tries to make my eyes meet his. "The world is lucky to have you."

We stare at each other for a bit. "No one has ever been so thoughtful to do everything you have, so thank you. It means a lot." I run my fingertips on the top of his hand.

"Besides the world, I'm lucky to have you as well. This is nothing compared to what I wish to do for you."

'Head in the Clouds' by Joji starts playing in the background. "I love this song."

"This is my favorite song, too. Like in the song, you make me feel like I'm in the clouds, Zara...and I just don't want to come down from it."

I know I was a bit emotional for a moment there...but hearing this is bringing up all the feelings that I felt at the bar and I just can't hold it in anymore. I put my hand on the back of his head, look him in the eyes and pull him close. He touches the sides of my waist, making his way to my back. He's staring at me, and I at him...and we both close our eyes. We don't hold ourselves back, and press our lips against each other. This is it...these are the sparks I had been imagining. Our kiss is so passionate, it's as if we had been craving each other for a lifetime. His hands make his way down my back, he lifts me and presses my body up against the wall. I pull his face even closer while we kiss. I can't get enough. His lips are intoxicating - sweet and soft. He works his mouth down my neck. I feel his lips brushing against my skin, sending shivers down my body.

We make our way over to the bedroom. He puts me down on the bed, and climbs on top of me. I run my hands underneath his shirt, he kneels up and undoes the buttons slowly without breaking eye contact. As he slides it off, I can see the definition of his body. He's more muscular than I expected. God took his sweet time making every inch of him. He pulls off my shirt and I lay there topless as he admires my body. He leans down and kisses me, starting at my lips and working his way down further, until he reaches my pj bottoms. He slides them down, and starts kissing up my legs until he reaches my inner thigh. He looks up at me and I bite my bottom lip and give him a nod. With a smile, he takes me in his mouth. I've never felt anything so amazing in my life and I can't help but let out a soft moan. I pull his face up and bring his lips to mine.

I don't know what's gotten into me but I push him onto his back and proceed to unbuckle his belt. I undo his pants slowly, letting him take in the warmth of my hands. I take them off of him and kiss my way up just as he did. Then, I take him in my mouth and look him in the eyes. I get a thrill off of how his body reacts. He sits up, and lifts me until I'm sitting in his lap. He flips me around so that he is laying on top of me, as I wrap my legs around him. We continue kissing, while his body rubs against mine. I push him up until he is kneeling over me. I open the right hand drawer like Jace told me to and take one out. He takes it out of my hand and rips it open with his mouth and places it onto himself. I feel his hand run down my inner thighs and push them apart. We make eye contact and I give him another nod letting him know I'm ready to give myself fully to him. I can feel him inside of me, as he moves his hips gently. He comes down to kiss me and I get a rush of pleasure. It is utter and complete euphoria and the world around me melts away. At this moment it's just us two, here and now.

CHAPTER EIGHT

Broken Heart Syndrome

THUD! I wake up to the sound of the door closing. I look to my left, and AJ is gone. Did he just leave? No, he can't just leave like that without telling me. He wouldn't do that. I get out of bed, put on my pj bottoms and shirt and walk over to the living room. He's not here but his jacket is still on the couch right where he left it last night. I check the bathroom, and he's not there either. I get this uneasy feeling...was this some sort of one night stand for him? I think to call him, but I realize I don't have his number. I grab my phone to call Jace and see that it's barely seven in the morning. Why did he leave so early and why without telling me?

***

It's around one in the afternoon, and I hear the door open. I don't even know when I fell back asleep. I head out to the living room and see Jace and Ari.

"Hey, love!" Ari springs to hug me.

"Hi, lovebirds." I try to conceal my low spirit from the two of them.

"Did you have fun last night?" Jace asks in his usual joking way, probably expecting an excited response from me.

"I did, yeah." I display a very deceptive smile, hoping Jace doesn't catch it.

"I'm gonna head to the shower, and then I'll see my favorite girls in a bit. Don't miss me too much!" He kisses Ari on the forehead, and heads to the bathroom while we make our way to the couch.

"I know he's my brother and all...but did you two, you know?" She winks.

I laugh uncomfortably, not knowing what to say. "Uh, well. I mean, between you and me, yeah." I don't know if I'm allowed to tell her or not, but it's not like AJ left a list of 'do's and don'ts'.

"Finally! This boy, I swear is all about work and no romance. He really likes you, Zara. I can tell."

Is she sure about that? Because right about now, I'm questioning him.

"Ari, he left his jacket here. Do you mind giving it to him?" I pick up the jacket and hand it to her.

"Why don't you give it to him yourself?"

"I don't know about that..."

She looks concerned after I say that.

"Do you not want to?"

"No, I do!" I try to change my tone. " I just thought it'd be easier if you gave it to him since you'd see him later, I'm assuming."

"Oh...do you guys not have plans today?"

"Not that I know of. He left early in the morning without telling me." Shit, I feel like I shouldn't have said that.

"That's so weird, it doesn't even sound like him. He didn't even try to wake you up before he left?"

I think back to make sure that I didn't miss that detail, but I feel like I would have remembered if he attempted to. "No, not that I remember."

"Maybe he had to leave early because he has rehearsals for the show. I wouldn't worry about it, love."

91

I can tell she's trying to comfort me with her words, but it's not working too well. "I'm surprised he went out last night. Usually, it's just me and him so even if he's recognized by someone, he doesn't worry about rumors spreading because I'm his sister and there's no restrictions to seeing family. He hasn't even hung out with his friends since he debuted, just his group members."

"So, what would happen if hypothetically he were to be seen with me, or any other girl?" I hope to get some sort of answer to ease my doubts.

"He doesn't really talk much about his contract with the company, or anything of that sort but I do know that if there is a rumor that makes the company look bad, there are consequences. I mean, him hanging out with you could be a potential problem, but I just assume he can cover it up."

Well, that's no help. I don't even think she's sure herself.

"He said something like, he's not supposed to be out. Apparently, he's been lying to his manager about going out to see me, and his group members have been lying to cover for him." Guilt hits me as I say that. I start to feel really bad.

"So, what if he lied? I swear, these K-Pop production companies act as if it's a crime to have a life outside of music. They can stick it where the sun doesn't shine for all I care!"

That made me feel a little less guilty, somehow. I mean, it's not like he's committing a murder by seeing me.

"I would feel terrible if he got in trouble and has to pay consequences for hanging out with me."

"Honestly, Zara. If I were you, I wouldn't feel guilty. He's really responsible, he always has been, but he's way too responsible. He thinks about others more than himself. I was actually so happy to hear about you. For once, he did something that made him happy."

That made me smile a little knowing I brought some sort of happiness into his life.

I try to change the subject from me to her. "Anyways, how was YOUR night?"

"It was amazing. Let's just say, you weren't the only one who had fun." I love how spirited she is. I should feel a little uncomfortable knowing that she knows I banged her brother last night, but she doesn't make it awkward at all.

"Yes!" I give her a high-five. "I'll let you in on a little secret." I move closer to her.

"Yes, tell me!"

"Jace is totally head over heels for you."

Her face illuminates with a smile. "You think so?!"

"Mhmm."

"Zara...I absolutely adore him. I know it's too soon to say, but I might be falling in love with him."

"Awe, really?!" That was so heartwarming to hear.

"Yeah. He's like...another me."

"Amen, sister. I saw that the minute I met you."

"I'm actually so sad that you guys are leaving in a few days. I wish I could just freeze time."

"You and me, both." I didn't want to think about that. It already hurts so much.

Jace walks out of the bathroom, and notices our gloom faces immediately. "Uh, I left this room with two chirpy women and walked back in as if someone had died."

Ari gets up, and gives him a bear hug.

"Wait, no one died, right?"

"No...we both just got sad that you and I have to leave in a few days."

"I know...but hey, we will see each other again!" He lifts Ari's chin and kisses her.

"We just have to make the most of the time we have together." She hugs him tighter as she says that. "Speaking of...Zara, you need to give him the jacket, yourself. You can surprise him!" She breaks out of Jace's arms. "I'll text him saying that I'll be stopping by to give him his jacket, but really it will be you! Oh, it will make him so happy."

Somehow, I get a feeling like this isn't a good idea.

"Are you sure?" I ask.

"Yes. one hundred percent! Just text me when you're outside the building. I'll then shoot him a text to come outside, and BAM! He'll be surprised. Here, give me your phone and I'll add my number." I hand my phone over. "Go get ready!"

"Alright, alright. I'm going!" I slightly laugh. I go to the room, grab my clothes and head to the bathroom. A part of me is excited to see him but the other part doesn't know what to expect after this morning.

***

I'm standing outside the building and my heart is racing. I text Ari to tell her I'm here. I anxiously look around me to see if there are people. Only a few, thankfully. I just can't seem to shake this feeling off that something bad is going to happen. The door opens...and it's not him. I don't know why, but I feel an instant relief. The door opens again after a few seconds, except this time, it's him. I recognize his eyes since he's wearing a face mask. His eyes widen and he stops walking forward. He's surprised alright, I just don't think it's in a good way.

"Uh, what are you doing here?" He starts looking around at our surroundings.

"You left your..." and before I finish my sentence, I find myself being dragged into this small parking garage that is next to the building. We stop by these stairs that are lit by a small light fixture on the wall.

"Why did you come?" He takes off his mask. His tone is not as loving as it was last night.

"You left your jacket at the hotel." I pull out his jacket from my bag.

He looks at it, and takes it from my hand. "I could have picked it up."

"Well, I gave it to Ari but she thought it would be a nice surprise if I came down to give it to you instead. Clearly, she was wrong." I scoff.

"You just...shouldn't have come here." He's being such an ass.

"Yeah, you made that clear." I turn around and start walking away.

"Wait." He grabs my hand.

"What?" I hope he senses how irritated and confused I am.

"I can't do this." He looks away.

"Do what?" I feel a rush of heat filling my head.

"This. Whatever this is."

I'm in disbelief. Did he really just say that?!

"Whatever this is?!" He stays quiet. I start feeling sick to my stomach. "What the hell are you talking about?"

"This was incredibly irresponsible of me."

"Oh, you mean seeing me, huh? Is that why you tiptoed your way out this morning?"

"Yeah..." He can't even look me in the eyes.

"You know, AJ. I may have asked you out in the first place, but you could have easily said no." My chest tightens. "Why didn't you just say no?!"

"I wasn't thinking!" He raises his voice.

"Yeah, you weren't!" I feel a lump in my throat.

"I'm sorry, it wasn't supposed to get this far."

"Get this far? I don't even know what you're trying to say!"

"You're leaving in a few days, Zara! What were you expecting?"

"I wasn't expecting you to be such a damn ass!" I couldn't hold my anger in any longer.

"I'm not being an ass. I'm being realistic! I can't betray my group, my fans! I have so much on the line. Besides, your life is in LA, mine is here." I'm incredibly distraught hearing all these words coming out of his mouth.

"No, really?! That thought didn't even occur to me at all!" I can feel my heart pound even faster and louder. "What happened from last night till now? It's like, you're a completely different person."

"Reality hit me! I wasn't supposed to stay over last night. Even at the bar, I stayed back when you helped that man because I had to lie about where I was going. I couldn't risk being recognized."

"And reality hit you right after we slept together?!" I let out a scornful laugh. "I get it. You just thought, oh this girl is leaving soon, might as well get a quick fling out of it!"

"No, it's not like that!" He tries to defend himself

"It totally is! You think I sleep with just anyone?! I thought you were different...I thought we had something special."

"I..." I interrupt him before I even hear the end of his sentence.

"And BY THE WAY, you're the one who asked me to come to the bar. YOU! You asked to see me again, not me!" I want to punch my hand through a wall.

"I know, and that was stupid of me."

"Incredibly stupid." There's a moment of silence between us.

"I didn't lie about how I felt."

"Tell it to someone who cares." I turn around and start walking away but I stop. My mind is telling me to keep walking, but my heart is saying to give him the last piece of my mind. "And to think...that I was falling in love with you. What a fucking fool I am." I turn back around, still feeling unsatisfied and start walking away fast. My heart is aching, my eyes can't hold back the tears. I feel like there's not enough oxygen in this damn country to fill up my lungs! He ripped my heart out, just like that. So much for Jace having faith in him...so much for ME having faith in him.

CHAPTER NINE

The Concert

I shut the door behind me, taking all of my anger, frustration and heartache out on it. I throw the hotel key so aggressively, it misses the table and lands on the floor. I can't even think straight, let alone walk without wanting to just crumble and break down on the ground. I lie on the bed, and let the tears stream down even more than they had on my walk back here.

How can a person completely change like that so quickly? I thought I had an idea of who he was, but I was wrong! He WAS too good to be true. Why was I so stupid to trust someone I just met?! I should have picked up on all the signs. As I'm self-criticizing more and more, I hear my phone ring. I jump out of bed, slightly hoping that it's AJ. But, it's only wishful thinking. It's my Mom. I don't need to feel more shitty than I already am! I wipe my tears, take a deep breath and press accept.

"Hello?" I answer, holding back my tears that are pushing to make their exit.

"Hi, Zara beta. How are you?"

God, why did she have to ask me that? Anyone who asks how you are when you're already crying, makes you want to cry even more!

"I'm good, Mom. How are you?"

"I'm good, too...are you sure okay?" Her motherly instincts cue in.

"Yeah, just tired."

"Hmm...Zara, you can talk to me. Did something happen?"

I can't hold it in and I burst into tears.

"I just...I got hurt!" I can't even speak in clear sentences. "A friend of mine, hurt my feelings really badly, and I was an idiot enough to trust them so much!"

"Oh, Zara. Do you want me to come over? I can if you want."

"No, no. I'll be okay. My friends and Jace are here to cheer me up."

"I'm so sorry. It's always the ones that we trust the most that end up hurting us, but don't let it bring down your faith in people."

"My faith in people was brought down a long time ago. This was just a small wake-up call." I hear Jace struggling to open the door, and then walk in. I quickly hide my face from his sight, and wipe my nose and eyes on the sleeve of my shirt. "Mom, I miss you. I have to go but I'll see you soon. I love you." This phone call didn't help but made me feel even more guilty about coming here without telling my parents. Maybe this heartbreak is my punishment.

"Oh, okay. You can call me if you need anything, Zara. I love you, too. Khuda-hafiz."

"Khuda-hafiz." I hang up. I look back at Jace, and his facial expression changes when he sees my face.

"Oh my God, Zara. Are you okay?" He rushes to my side.

"Yeah, I just..." I stop to think. I shouldn't tell him what happened between AJ and I. I wouldn't want to ruin things between him and Ari. "I just feel really guilty that I hid this from my parents, and I think it just overwhelmed me when I heard Mom's voice."

He places my head on his shoulder. "No, no, my dear. Remember what we talked about on the plane? Living in the moment! That's what this trip was all about. "

If only he knew that's what got me into this mess.

"I know what you need. How does hot chocolate and some pastries sound? We need to get into the holiday spirit! Completely forgot Christmas is in a few days."

"Oh, wow. I forgot about it, too. I wait all year for it."

"And this year, you got a Christmas gift without even asking for it!"

He laughs and I slightly die inside. Not talking about AJ to Jace is going to be harder than I thought.

***

It's been two days since I last saw AJ. I thought he would have called by now to apologize, or something. Anything! I leave tomorrow...does he really not care to even say goodbye? It's been extremely hard to keep a straight face when Jace mentions his name. It's going to be harder to see him perform tonight. The sad thing is, even after all that...I still want to see him. I know I probably won't get to talk to him, but at least I'll get to see him one last time.

"Excited to see AJ tonight?" Jace asks while he checks out the souvenirs at a small shop we found around the corner.

"Uh, yeah. I can't wait." God, how long am I going to keep this from him?

"You two haven't hung out in the past two days. Is everything okay?"

"Yeah, it's just...he's really busy with rehearsals and I didn't want to distract him. It seems to be a big show."

"So, he can't even take out an hour to see you? He knows you're leaving tomorrow, right?"

I can see he's a little suspicious.

"Yeah, he does but I told him that he should focus on rehearsals and that I'll just spend time with him after the concert. Plus, I wanted to spend more time with you."

"But, he hasn't even called. I haven't seen you talk to him one bit."

Shit, what do I say? "Yeah, um...it's okay. I honestly don't mind."

"Don't mind? You basically couldn't shut up about this guy two days ago, and now you just DON'T mind?" He furrows his eyebrows.

"Jace, it's not a big deal." I start getting a little annoyed.

"I feel like you're hiding something from me, and usually it's the other way around."

"I'm not hiding anything!"

"Why are you being so defensive? You're acting REALLY weird, and it's pissing me off."

I take a deep breath and try to calm down. "I'm sorry, Jace." I hug him. "I guess I'm just a little anxious about getting home."

He runs his fingers through my hair. "We'll get home safely, I promise you. If there's anything that's on your mind, I don't want you hiding it from me. That's not what we do."

I close my eyes and squeeze him tighter. "I know." I sigh. "Anyways, we should wrap up here and get a bite to eat before we head back to get ready."

"Okay, yeah. You know I love you, right? I'm always here for you."

"I know you are." I flick his nose and make a silly face at him. I wish I didn't have to hide this but I'm not willing to ruin his relationship over my heartbreak.

"Wow, there are a lot of people here to see your boyfriend." Jace and I are standing outside of Olympic Hall where the concert is held. There are crowds of really young people - especially girls - giggling their way inside the venue. A lot of them are wearing t-shirts with the members' faces, decorated with hearts and stars. It made me a little sick seeing AJ's face, which is basically everywhere. I'm trying really hard to put on a smile and just enjoy the concert for Jace's sake, but it's taking me back to that agonizing conversation he and I had. I just want to get through this, go back to the hotel, pack and get the hell out of Korea. Or, just pray that this was all a dream, and wake up in my bed, snuggled up with my pillow.

"Jace, shut up! Oh my God, don't say it out loud."

"Or what? Who here is going to believe it? He's practically everyone's boyfriend here, well in their minds." He's right, from the looks of it, all of these girls are in a parasocial relationship with him. We get through security and head to our seats. Thankfully, our seats are close to the exit and far from the stage, which saves me the trouble of seeing his gorgeous, stupid face up close.

"Ari is backstage. We can go there if you want?"

"Um, no. I'm okay here, but you're more than welcome to go." I don't want to hold him back from enjoying the concert.

"I'm not gonna leave you alone! We can just meet up with them after the concert."

Shit, I should just tell him what happened. It would be so awkward if I end up seeing AJ after with Ari and Jace around. I can't pretend nothing happened.

I can't help but feel the anticipation as we move from one act to the other. With every performance getting closer and closer to AJs', I don't know how I'll feel once he comes on stage. I have to tell Jace right now.

"Jace, I need to tell..."

"Bitch, shut up, there's your boyfriend!" The whole crowd starts cheering, and girls are screaming their lungs out when AJ comes out on stage. Following him, the group members come out one by one.

"Hello, beautiful people! We are...NOWus!"

AJ is very energetic on stage like Jace said. The audience is going wild. I swear, I think I saw a girl nearby take off her shirt and start crying hysterically out of happiness. Where the hell am I?! Maybe this is the normal at concerts, I wouldn't know...this is probably my second concert I've been to since the one that was held back in college when Ella Mai came.

"These people are cheering more for your boyfriend than you! What kind of girlfriend are ya?!" Jace shouts in my ear since it's so overbearingly loud.

I can't even hear my own heartbeat.

"He's not my boyfriend!"

"What?! I can't hear you!"

"He's not...nevermind!" I give up. I'm not about to lose my voice right now. I start clapping along with the crowd and swaying side to side with Jace. I figured I should just fake it till I make it...out of here!

I won't lie, the lights, and the special effects were a sight to see. I can see what the fuss is about. Even from the back of the auditorium, I feel like I'm standing right in front of him. They're amazing performers to say the least. Seeing his group all together takes me back to the argument we had. Before I didn't understand where he was coming from, but I do now. I get why he feels irresponsible. It's not just his career that he's putting in jeopardy, but also theirs. Being here and seeing him perform puts everything into perspective through his eyes. He would be losing ALL of this just by one careless act. Of course, it doesn't make this any less painful, especially seeing him right now. So close to me but also so far from my grasp.

They announce that they're playing their last song. Finally. Then I can leave in peace and never have to think about him again. Well, I probably will think about him from time to time but I don't think I'll ever be in a situation where I'll see him again unless Jace marries Ari. Ah, but Jace wants to see Ari after the concert backstage, and...he will be there! I just need to blurt it out..

"Jace, I can't go backstage with you."

He doesn't stop swaying to the music. "Why?"

"Well, something happened between me and AJ."

"What do you mean?"

And right when he asks me, AJ starts giving his closing statement and the screaming fans go at it again, but this time even louder.

"When I went to give AJ his jacket..."

"Zara, speak louder, I can't hear you!"

"WHEN I WENT TO SEE AJ..."

"What?!"

There is no way he can hear me . I shake my head, mouthing 'nothing' but he doesn't look away. His eyes are stuck on me. I think he can notice something is off. I'm trying to think of a way to tell him but then AJ stops talking. We both turn our eyes back to the stage. AJ is standing still, looking towards the ground. His group members are looking at him, and then at each other. The fans stop screaming and wait for him to start speaking again. Everyone is equally as confused as I am right now. He looks back up at the crowd, and starts talking.

"I learned a really valuable lesson in the past few days, and I want to pass it along to you guys."

My heart drops. There's no way he's talking about me, is he?

"I hurt a very dear friend's feelings and ever since then, I've been feeling really down and it hasn't sat right with me."

Okay, he has to be talking about me, unless there is someone else he hurt as well, which in that case he really needs to get his shit together.

"This friend...means a lot to me, and I know is out here somewhere tonight. I think at times we say hurtful things that we don't mean to those we really care about. Sometimes it's a defense mechanism. Whatever it is, I know what I said to my friend, I didn't want to say. I didn't mean any of it, but I think I did damage that cannot be reversed."

God, he is talking about me. My eyes unwillingly start tearing up. I want to just run up to him, and give him the biggest hug I can, but at that moment, I realize some of the things he said weren't wrong.

"To that friend, I'm really sorry. I wish I could say this to you while you stand in front of me, but I don't know if I will get to do that. I'll miss you."

Why did he have to say all this?! At least his hurtful words could have been a form of assurance that what we had wasn't real, making it easier to move on from him. But, instead he said the right words at the wrong time. My heart cannot take this right now. I start sobbing quietly, but Jace sees it.

"Zara, what the..." The confusion on his face speaks for itself.

"Jace, I can't be here right now." I lower my head down, and walk fast towards the exit.

"Zara, wait! Where the hell are you going?!" Jace grabs my arm and pulls me close to him. "He was talking about you, wasn't he?" His nostrils flare and his jaw clenches. "What the hell did he do? Tell me right now!"

"He...said it was a...a whatever, I don't know!" The words won't come out. I'm feeling a roller coaster of emotions, and hearing him apologize like that...I realized how temporary this happiness is. Tomorrow, I'll be heading back to reality...and man, I will miss him and this trip so much that it physically hurts.

"There you guys are! I saw you two run out as I was coming over..." Ari ends her sentence when she sees me. "Oh my God, Zara, what happened?" She places her hand on my back, and looks at Jace for an explanation.

"Ask your brother." Jace answers angrily.

God, this is why I didn't want to tell him.

"No, it's nothing, Ari. Please don't worry about it. AJ and I just got into a small argument, but it's fine."

"Zara...you can tell me, I will literally kill him right now." Great, I've turned her against her own brother. That just makes me feel even worse.

"No, Ari. Please don't say anything to him. I just...I can't be here right now."

"Okay, lets go." Jace starts walking.

"No." I stop him in his tracks. "I need to be alone, Jace. I love you for this, but please be with Ari. It's our last night here, and I will feel even worse if you don't spend it with her."

"Zara, we both can come with you." Ari pulls me close for a hug.

"Please. Both of you. I know you guys want to comfort me, but I just have to be alone. You two please, have fun, go enjoy your night." I kiss Ari on the cheek. "I will miss you, Ari. Merry Christmas." We both smile, and I see her eyes becoming glossy as if she's about to cry. "I'm going to head to the hotel, I already ordered an Uber." I lied, I hadn't yet. "See you back at the hotel, Jace. Don't rush." I calm myself down just so the worry on his face goes away. This was the last thing I wanted.

I step outside, and order an Uber. My tears well up again, but I don't even bother to do anything about it. The cold breeze, the night sky, the moon...everything was just reminding me of the time I spent with AJ and without a doubt in my mind...I fell deeply and utterly in love with him.

***

"Zara? Did you get to the hotel?" I can hear Ari in the back asking him how I'm doing.

"Yeah, I got back thirty minutes ago." I sniffle while packing all my belongings in the suitcase. I was hoping it would distract in some way, but failed.

"We met up with AJ after you left...he told us what happened." My makeup bag slips out of my hand. I wasn't expecting them to meet up. "I may have yelled at him a little, but I can tell he genuinely feels really sorry. He said he wants to see you."

"I can't, Jace. I don't think I'll be able to handle it. He wasn't wrong. It just seems that reality just hit him sooner than me. Honestly, it's probably just best that I didn't get to talk to him tonight, seeing him would just break my heart even more than it already is."

"Oh, well...the thing is I think he's on his way to see..." right then, I hear a knock on the door. My blood turns cold.

"Jace...are you at the door?" I ask, even though I already have a feeling it's not him.

"Just answer the door. Trust me." He hangs up. I walk towards the door, contemplating whether or not I should open it.

"Zara, I know you're in there. Open the door, please."

His voice feels like a punch to the gut.

"Please. Open the door."

I can hear the desperation and stay quiet, not being able to think or breathe.

"I'm sorry. I'm so fucking sorry. Please... just open up." I reach for the handle but then stop.

Through the door, I ask, "I want to. I really do...but what would be the point?"

"The point...I don't know, Zara! I just know that I need to see you, hold you, kiss you. We can't end like this! I need to see your face, and explain myself! I didn't mean any of it, I just...I fucked up!" He clears his throat as his voice starts to crack.

"No, you were right, AJ! You were just stating the inevitable."

"I was wrong! I didn't know what the hell I was saying. You have to understand, I've never been in this position before. I've always been so responsible, but then you came along and I stopped caring about the rules! Zara, I don't think you realize how happy you have made me in the past few days. It's like...I didn't care if I got in trouble. I didn't care about anything else...I just got lost in this happiness I've never felt before. After that night, I guess it hit me that I would do anything for you. I freaked out and was scared!"

"I hear you, AJ. I really do. I wish you had said this earlier but...you shouldn't have to change who you are for me. I mean, you were right! I live in LA, you live here. But, also our lives are completely different. I could never be a part of your life, and you could never be a part of mine. We don't fit!"

"We fit perfectly. Zara...the things I shared with you, I've never had the courage to be this vulnerable with anyone else. This connection we have, it's something that I've only heard others talk about. I never thought I'd be able to experience it for myself. This has to be something worth holding on to, right?"

I want to say yes, it is worth holding on to but I can't let him sacrifice everything he has worked so hard for just to be with me.

My hand still rests on the door knob. "But, reality will catch up to us sooner or later...and then this will all be over. I mean, maybe we are crazy. We have only known each other for what, a week?"

"You don't mean any of this! I know you don't. I know you're feeling how I felt two days ago and now you're just saying things to make this easier."

"No, I'm not. This is how I feel. You know, it's probably just best to leave it at this." I cover my mouth so he doesn't hear my cries.

"Don't say this, please. I know that's not how you feel."

"It doesn't matter how I feel."

"It matters to me! I...I love you, Zara!" My heart stops. I turn my back against the door, and slide down in tears. "Please don't do this!"

"It's already done!"

I hear him crumble to the floor.

I want to open the door so badly and hold him as I hear the sobs escape his mouth. We sit there in silence, until I hear him get up. Without a word, he starts to walk away...chipping at my heart with every fading footstep, until there is nothing left.

CHAPTER TEN

The Departure

"Here's your passport." Jace hands it to me. He's been quite avoidant all morning. I know he's trying to give me my space but he's probably dying to hear the details from last night. "I got you hot chocolate and a croissant while you were packing."

"Thanks, Jace."

"Yeah, no problem." He clears his throat. "So, uh, are you ready to leave?"

My heart still feels shattered. It's as if I'm leaving a piece of myself here. "Yeah, ready as I'll ever be." I force a smile.

"Zara...I'm sorry."

"No, it's okay. I'm okay."

"You're not okay. I know you're not. Do you want to talk about it?"

"No, not really. Right now, we need to get our stuff together and leave for the airport." I don't want to think about last night, or anything that has to do with AJ. I just want to get home and try to forget everything about him, although that seems impossible.

"We're going to have to talk about it sooner or later." He grabs my bag from me and sets it by the door.

"Yeah, now is not the time though."

Jace looks at his phone. "Uber's here. You have everything?"

I gaze around, and as I do, I am flooded by the memories that took place in this room. If I could stay in this room and relive those moments, I would. It's almost as if I became attached to it...just like I am to AJ. We make our way out of the room, I turn back around and take one last glance. "Yup, everything." God, I already miss Korea.

***

"Ladies and gentlemen, please fasten your seatbelts. We will be taking off shortly, thank you."

I got the window seat, and Jace got the aisle. As I look out the window, I reminisce about the day we arrived. I didn't know how much my life would change once I stepped foot in this country. It feels like I've already lived a lifetime here. AJ's face kept appearing in front of my eyes. It's as if I photographed his exact details in my mind. His smile, his dimples, his laugh...I don't think I'll ever forget anything about him.

The plane starts moving. The captain turns on the seatbelt sign. I wanted to unbuckle mine, and run out. It's like I'm fighting against my own heart, but I'm leaving it here with AJ. My eyes fill with tears and fall as the plane starts moving. Will I ever see him again? Did I make a mistake by not letting him in last night? The plane goes faster, and faster, then takes off. The wheels tuck inside the belly, and I see the city below me get smaller and smaller. I cover my mouth, and let my tears fall freely. This pain is indescribable.

Jace places his hand on mine. "Zara..."

"I'm okay." I speak slowly so my voice doesn't crack.

"You're not okay. Zara, You need to talk about this. How do you really feel?"

"I...don't want to talk about it."

"Pretend I'm AJ, and tell me what you would want to tell him."

"I don't want to tell him anything, Jace. What I wanted to say to him, I said last night."

"I feel like you didn't tell him how you truly felt. Did you?"

I shrug. "It doesn't matter."

"Come on, I promise this exercise will help. Talk to me as if I'm AJ."

"Jace, I don't want..." Suddenly, the plane jolts and the lights flicker.

"What the hell was that?!" Jace looks around.

We start to feel major turbulence, and everyone gasps, grabbing their arm rests.

"Jace...what's going on?!" I can feel the plane starting to drop. I get the feeling when you're on a roller coaster, and at the sudden drops, your stomach feels like it's in your heart.

"Uh, I don't know but it's probably nothing." Jace tries to remain calm.

"This is your captain speaking. It seems like we are experiencing turbulence. Please remain in your seats."

"Okay, we are going to be fine. Must be the weather." I take a deep breath and pat Jace on his shoulder...but then, there's another drop.

"Oh, hell no. This doesn't seem right." Jace squeezes my hand.

"No, Jace, we will be fine! Look, it will stop going down any second!"

"This is your captain speaking. We are trying to fix the problem but until then, please stay calmly seated with your seatbelts on and put on the oxygen masks."

"Problem? Put on oxygen masks?!" I panic.

Immediately, the oxygen masks drop down to our laps, and everyone starts screaming. Children are crying and I can hear the person behind me praying. We are all trying to put on the masks as quickly as possible, but I'm having trouble. My hands keep shaking, my fingers won't work and a million thoughts are going through my head.

112

"Zara, wear your mask!" Jace yells.

"I'm trying, but my hands won't stop shaking!" Jace grabs the mask out of my hand, and places it over my mouth. "God, we can't be dying like this! This isn't how it was supposed to end!"

"We aren't dying, calm down!"

"Yes, we are! I think God was listening when I was having my mini meltdown, and suggested that my parents are going to find out about my trip by seeing me in a body bag. Jesus, I didn't think God would be okay with making every single person on this plane collateral damage!" I try to take deep breaths. "Jace...I should have said goodbye to him!"

"Okay, so it only took death to get you talking!" He holds onto his armrests as we speed downwards faster.

"I thought, you know, maybe we will cross paths in the future, somehow but clearly not! I'm such an idiot, I should have opened the door! I should have kissed him! Jace, I can't believe I just stood there while he said I love you!"

"He said what?!" The shock on Jace's face makes me forget the plane is about to crash.

"He said he loves me! HE LOVES ME! And what did I do?! I didn't say a word! I told him to leave!" I start crying again. "I should have said it! I should have told him how I feel about him!"

"How do you feel about him?!" He asks while looking at the lights that continue flickering.

"I love him! I love him so much!" The pressure of the plane gets stronger, I look outside and we are close to the ground. Oh, God! It's getting closer and closer! I close my eyes and hold onto Jace, preparing for what's next.

"Zara! Wake the hell up."

I get up and look around frantically. "What happened? Did we crash?"

He has a confused look on his face. "Uh, no. Thankfully, we haven't crashed. You have been sleeping for the past hour, since we took off actually. Then, you started screaming out of nowhere."

"What, really?" When the hell did I fall asleep?

"Yeah...you started crying and mumbling in your dream. It was freaking me out so I woke your dumb ass up."

I sit up straight. "I had the craziest dream."

"Was it a sex one?" He squeezes his eyes shut. "Shit, I know, too soon? I'm sorry."

"No, it wasn't that. You were forcing me to open up about what happened, and then our plane started going down and was about to crash, and that's when I started confessing how I felt."

"Wow, that's a scary ass dream. Thanks for telling me that, now I won't be able to sleep." He chuckles. "What did you confess?"

I shake my head and sigh. "Just something I feel like I should have said to AJ."

"And, what is that?"

"That I love him." It's weird hearing those words escape my mouth. Both Jace and I are in a bit of a shock as I said it.

"You do, huh? I thought this was just infatuation for you but...I can tell you fell really hard for him." He softens his voice.

"I really did. I mean, this is crazy to think about, you know? It's been like a week since I met him, and so quickly I fell in love. Who knows, maybe it's not love but...everything I felt this week makes it feel as if this is exactly how it should feel like."

"I think it was love. I could tell by the way you two looked at each other."

"I can't stop thinking about him, Jace. I regret not opening the door and seeing him. I thought it would just make things harder...harder to leave him behind. It just feels worse that I didn't get to see him. What if it was the last time I ever saw him? That thought breaks my heart."

114

"It won't be. Zara, I have a feeling both of your paths will cross one day."

"You think so?"

"I do. Even if the universe tries to keep you two from seeing each other, you or AJ will fight against it. If you think you gained nothing from this trip but a heartbreak, you're wrong. You got to feel emotions you had never before. You aren't the same person you were before coming to Korea. You allowed yourself to be vulnerable and open...two things that are hard for you to do. Look how far you've come along in such a short period of time. Maybe he's supposed to be a small chapter in your life, but it was a great one...one that you'll look back at as fond memories. The best memories tend to be the most painful because you can't relive them again. But, you'll make even better ones and who knows...it might be with him."

"It just hurts so much, Jace. You're right, I do want to turn back time to a week ago and run into him over and over again. What if I never feel this way about anyone else ever again? But then I think, I have to get over these feelings eventually. The truth is...I couldn't be a part of his world, and he can't be a part of mine. I'd love to see my parents reaction if I told them their son-in-law would be a non-Pakistani Muslim. My community would have a field day with that one."

"You think your parents wouldn't approve of him?"

"No, I don't think so. That makes me feel a little better, in some weird way. It's like a better reason for us not to be together, knowing there wasn't an option there to begin with. Then, there are his reasons which are equally as bad."

"If you could tell him anything right now, without any other influences, what would you say?"

I don't even hesitate to think about it because I know my answer. "I would say that he is worth holding on to. What we felt...it was pure and real. Being around him was like time had stopped and it was just the two of us on this planet. I'd tell him if I didn't have to worry about what my parents would say,

I'd make him mine in a heartbeat...and never let go. I'd give us a chance because I'm so hopelessly in love with him."

Jace wraps his arm around me. "You'll say this to him one day, I have a strong feeling."

"I hope you're right. I thought about calling him once we land."

"Well, will you?"

"No. I'm not going to. I figured I shouldn't make things harder for either one of us. He'll move on. Let's not forget, he is a famous K-Pop star. He'll have a new girl by next week and forget all about me."

"Yeah...I don't think he's the type to move on that easily. No guy makes that much effort for a girl he doesn't like. Trust me...when I spoke to him after the concert, he wasn't okay. "

"What do you mean?" My curiosity grew.

"He literally grabbed me and started asking where you were. I felt like I was in an interrogation room. He just kept saying how afraid he was of losing you. It's not something someone would say if they were playing around."

"I know...I'm just trying to make myself feel better."

"Is it working?"

"No, not really."

"Then stop thinking stupid shit. Just hold on to this love you both shared and cherish it. You got to live out this love story that is only written in books and shown in movies. A lot of people don't get to experience what you did."

He's right. Everything that happened on this trip is comparable to a fantasy. I know it sounds strange, but it's like I grew a lot during this trip. Perhaps what happened was for the best...or maybe it wasn't, who knows. I don't regret any of it anymore.

Not even one bit.

***

"I'm exhausted!" Jace sets down our luggage by our apartment door while I look through my bag - which is STILL a mess- to find the keys.

"If only you'd let me help you with the suitcases, you wouldn't be as tired."

"Have you seen your arms? They're like twigs. They would break in a second and I wasn't up for making a trip to the hospital."

"They're not THAT bad. Where the hell are those keys?!" I start moving around all the junk that is filled in my bag and then I drop it. It was like deja vu, reminding me of my first date with AJ, except no condoms fell out this time.

"Found them!" Jace picks up the keys from the ground. "You need to clean out that bag."

"Yeah...and the rest of my baggage, too." We both laugh and head inside. While it feels good to be back home, it doesn't feel the same. Maybe because I'm not the same person as I was when I left. I start unpacking as soon as I get to my room, dumping out all my clothes from the suitcase. The NASA shirt, the blue dress, the jewelry I wore on our dates...it's painful to even look at these now without thinking about how those memories. I stuff them back in and shove the suitcase against the wall. Yeah, I cannot do this right now. Unpacking can wait a day or two.

"You okay, baby girl?" I come out to the living room and find Jace sipping on a beer while watching Friends on Netflix.

"Yeah, just can't unpack right now without thinking about...you know who."

"Ah, okay. Come here." He opens his arm. I snuggle next to him while he runs his fingers through my hair.

"I wish I could just have a car accident and forget AJ."

"Bitch, why the hell would you wish that upon yourself?! You're willing to put your life at risk just so you can forget him? Hell no."

117

"Okay, maybe I'm a little dramatic here. You know what I mean. I could really use something cozy and warm right about now."

"Like, food?" He raises his eyebrow. The doorbell rings.

For a second, I thought it might be AJ. "Is that...AJ?"

"Oh...no. Sorry. I ordered your favorite takeout. I thought it would make you a little happy. Can you get the door? I'm gonna grab my wallet."

It was just wishful thinking, which left me just a tad bit disappointed. Food, on the other hand, does the complete opposite. "Yeah, I'll get it." I open the door, take the food from the delivery girl and set it on the dining table.

Jace takes out cash from his wallet. "They still there?"

"Yeah, I told her you're coming out with the money."

He opens the door. "Uh, Zara...can you come here for a second?" I set the plates down and head to him.

"What is it?" I turn to see what he's looking at.

"Hey, Zara."

I freeze in place.

"AJ..."

Acknowledgements

I want to thank my best friend, Jose Cuevas, for staying up late with me during most nights and going over each chapter, word by word. I always looked forward to that part of my day, when we'd FaceTime and spend hours going over the book, laughing till our stomachs hurt! You were such a big part of this whole journey, and I couldn't have done it without your support. I will cherish those memories forever.

I also want to thank my cousin-brother, Ibrahim Zaidi, for all of your input regarding the book. Thank you for taking the time out for me from your busy schedule. I couldn't have written this book without your wise words and informative feedback. Thank you for all the support and encouragement.

Thank you to my editor, Sarah Lamb, and designer, Emily, for being so patient with me!

Thank you, Mom, Dad, Taha, and Rafia for your love and support during this huge chapter of my life. I love you all.

About the Author

Misbah Zaidi was born and raised in Orange County, California. She attended the University of California, Irvine, earning a degree in Sociology. While she pursues a career in medicine, another passion of hers is writing. Growing up, she enjoyed reading a variety of books and immersing herself in fictional worlds. These books inspired her to create a fantasy of her own, Falling in Love in Korea, Misbah's first book.